GRAYSON

JASPER SPRINGS

BOOK FOUR

BY EVIE RILEY

Grayson

An MM Friends To Lovers Romance

Jasper Springs

Book Four

Copyright © 2024

Evie Riley

Second Edition

ISBN: 978-1-77357-687-9

Published by Naughty Nights Press LLC

Cover Art By Willsin Rowe

GRAYSON

A weekend of glamping.

A little too much wine tasting.

All inhibitions forgotten.

Grayson Sanderson can't escape the pressure from his parents to find someone to settle down with, especially with his sister's impending nuptials on the horizon. Despite his successful life running a bridal boutique, Grayson can't seem to find his own Prince Charming.

When a series of unfortunate events force Grayson to room with his sister's best friend's brother on the bridal party's weekend wine trip, Grayson finds himself in uncharted territory.

Henry Markell can't seem to catch a break anywhere. When his sister invites him to come along to her friend's bridal party weekend for some well needed luxury and relaxation, Henry thinks his luck is changing.

Until he discovers he's sharing a dome with the sexy and mysterious Grayson, who is more than out of his league. But Henry can't help wanting things he can't have.

Will Grayson give in to his dreams? Or will Henry's notorious bad luck get in the way once more?

Readers seeking a friends to lovers romance with forced proximity set in a cozy little town may find this story ticks that mark. While Grayson and Henry will have cameos in future stories, each book in this series can be read as a standalone.

CHAPTER ONE

Grayson

I SHOULD HAVE known that the offering of freshly poured coffee and scones would come with strings.

I mean, after all, this was my sister we were talking about.

"Please, Grayson, do it for me..." she whined, batting her long eyelashes at me, pouting like she used to do when we were kids.

I looked out the window of the cafe, sighing in exasperation because I knew I would inevitably give in. Because if I didn't, I'd never hear the end of it from her, my mother, and God knows who else. But that didn't mean I was going to go easy.

"You know I don't really care for the *bar scene,*" I said, my voice firm. But that never swayed Giselle.

"We have a month until the wedding, Grayson. Don't get squeamish now when we're in the home stretch."

I scoffed at her remark. "Excuse me for having *standards*, Giselle."

She crossed her arms, raising an eyebrow at me. "Impeccably *high* standards, might I add. You haven't even had a date in what? Three years?"

I bristled at her words. It wasn't like I *couldn't* get a date. Honestly, I knew if I wanted I could just swipe right on about anyone I fancied, but truth be told, there was far more pressure on me to "pick the perfect match" since I'd come out to my parents.

Which was Giselle's fault entirely.

Not to mention the dating scene, especially in this town, wasn't exactly the most private. When you lived in a small town like Jasper Springs, and your family was one of the most well-known, everyone and their brother was up in your business.

Including meddling, pain in the ass

siblings.

"It's different for me, and you know that," I said with a sigh, knowing my fate would be sealed soon enough.

To my surprise, my sister's gaze softened, her lips frowning slightly.

"Oh, Grayson, I didn't mean—"

"I know you didn't, but the fact of the matter is you know mom and dad hold me to a higher standard now."

"Like they didn't have high expectations for me? And Aaron?"

"Aaron's father is the CEO of a high-end realty company. There was never any doubt they'd love him," I said, wanting to veer away from this uncomfortable conversation.

I loved my sister, and she was one of the sweetest, most empathetic allies I knew. But regardless of how understanding or big her heart was, she'd never really understand my station. The oldest sibling, the one our parents expected would lead this family into the next era with a bunch of crotch dumplings, a total Betty for a wife, with a seven figure stock portfolio and a house in the Hamptons.

And I'd shattered all their dreams of

the perfect American family when they'd found out I was gay, in the worst way possible.

Caught red-handed with my tongue down my sister's high school ex-boyfriend's throat.

Talk about a scandal.

Our families knew each other well, and Cody and I just happened to be working at the same suit store at the time, and he and my sister seemed to be civil enough that inviting him and his family to the summer shindig was a no brainer, and it just sort of... happened.

After several martinis at the family bbq.

In the pool house.

Where we'd forgot to lock the door amidst nearly half the population of Jasper Springs, because we were drunk. But we'd been fucking around for weeks at that point.

Needless to say, the whole debacle was a nightmare, and when push came to shove, Cody clammed up and sang the tune of "He came on to me. I'm not gay."

I was forced to come clean and tell my parents the truth, much sooner than I'd wanted to.

Of course, I'd planned on telling them... eventually. When I found Mr. Right, and knew he was the one, so they'd never question me or my choice, but now...

Now my parents were looking for any reason to remind me of my bachelor status, my eternal singledom after what had happened with Cody.

"I'm sorry," I said, shaking my head as I dispelled the unforgiving, awful memories. "I'm just... All this wedding stuff is getting to my head, I think."

My sister squeezed my hand softly, forcing me to look at her pleading eyes, her sympathetic face.

"Does that mean you'll come? I promise it'll be fun. We've been so hell-bent on planning, I think we could all use a drink and some tunes, don't you?"

Damn it.

"Always a bridesmaid, never a bride," I said, flashing her with a smirk as I pulled my hand away. "Perhaps I could settle for *one* drink. But that is it! I swear, I—"

Giselle's smile brightened as she nodded in response. "Seven o'clock at M's Place. Don't be late."

CHAPTER TWO

Grayson

THE AIR SMELLED like stale nuts and beer, and I couldn't help but wrinkle my nose. I didn't much care for bars in general, but bars like M's Place were below even my lowest standards.

I didn't begrudge anyone for owning their own business, but the place could have most certainly used a more sophisticated Queer Eye to spruce the place up and make it more comfortable.

It didn't take long to find my sister and her wedding party, being as her laugh was like a dolphin call all on its own.

I made my way through the sea of folks, hot, sweaty bodies clamored together to watch one another drone out tone-deaf songs on stage.

I swear to god if someone sings Taylor Swift, I will lose my shit.

Casually, I strolled over to their two high tables pushed together.

"Grayson, so glad you could make it!" Mia said, coming over to give me a hug. While Giselle and I may not have run in the same circles, we spent a ton of time together outside of those circles, which meant sometimes there was overlap.

I hugged Mia, my gaze settling on the remainder of the party around the tables. Giselle's neighbor, Julie, and her friend slash florist, Taylor, her fiancé Aaron, the best man, Riley, and the most nauseating couple I'd ever met, Lacey and Lane.

Mia's earthy brown eyes sparkled in the low light as she smiled, pulling away.

"Yeah, well, I didn't really have much of a choice, now did I?" I whined, and everyone chuckled.

Giselle rolled her eyes, just as our server came to our table with a platter full of waters. My eyes widened as I recognized the man, if only from passing events.

"Hey, Henry! I'm so glad you could wait

on us tonight!" Mia said as she squealed with excitement at her brother.

Henry smiled affectionately, the corners of his lips turning up with, no doubt, practiced politeness.

His chocolate brown hair fell haphazardly into his amber eyes, his hand placed delicately on his hip as he greeted us.

I didn't know the man well, and the last time I'd truly seen him was at Giselle and Aaron's engagement party nearly four months ago.

He looked different, dressed down in a pair of jeans and a black *M's Place* shirt with an apron tied around his waist.

For some reason, my cock stirred as my gaze settled on said waist, on the slender, toned muscles of his arms that his tight uniform shirt only drew attention to.

"Henry," I drawled as his gaze caught mine.

"It's Grayson, right?" he asked as he tapped his pen against his book.

"It is," I said, shaking my head and dispelling all the weirdness that had somehow managed to set between us.

"What, uh, what it'll be?" he asked, his

tone casual, all business and no play.

"I'll have a gin martini, with extra olives, please," I said, leaning against the table, if only to try and stifle the erection that was forming in my pants from the sheer *sight* of this man.

The last time I'd seen him, he'd been dressed in a basic blue blazer and dress pants, dark hair slicked back like he was going to a school dance or something.

I'd thought he was cute then, like a little fish out water. He stood out like a sore thumb among the rest of the three hundred and fifty guests at the engagement party, but he'd also hung back.

I, of all people, understood being anti-social. Especially when you were being dragged to a wedding event against your will. So, I'd done the most noble thing I could do, and left him alone to his devices. I knew I much preferred if someone left *me* alone, but alas, being the brother of the bride and part of the wedding party had its disadvantages too.

"Coming..." he said, his voice cracking for a moment as he pulled at his collar. "...right up," he said, turning away from me, but not before I could see the flush of pink in his cheeks.

My gaze fell to his perfectly shaped ass in those tight blue jeans, and I had to admit, it looked divine walking away from me.

I broke away from the preferred sight, if only because I didn't want to seem like a total creeper.

Mia threw her arm around me, forcing me to look up, noting Giselle caught my gaze and raised an eyebrow at me.

"Tonight is going to be the best night ever!" Mia drawled as Lacey, Julie, and Giselle raised their water glasses in salute, and I was remiss to raise my own.

But when in Rome, one should do as the Romans do, right?

CHAPTER THREE

Henry

I SET MY SIGHTS on my sister and the other members of Giselle's party from behind the bar as I gathered waters for the table together, watching with perhaps a little bit of fear of missing out.

My sister, Mia, and Giselle had been friends for years, so it wasn't like it was unexpected that Giselle would have asked her to be a bridesmaid. What was unexpected was how Giselle constantly opened the invitation to me to join her and the wedding party at events that were deemed for the wedding party themselves. Like tonight, they had all decided they needed a "night out" and had decided to come to M's Place for the monthly Bar Bingo and Karaoke. Giselle texted me, as well as my sister, inviting me, but unfortunately I'd been called in to work due to a last minute call off. Which happened to be the very place they were going.

How embarrassing that I couldn't hang out with everyone because I would be the one *serving* them.

But I guess, in a way it was like I was still part of the group... even if I couldn't really hang out because I was working.

The party themselves was a decent size, and I recognized a few other individuals at their table, even though I knew they weren't part of the main party. Taylor, the local florist, and Giselle's GQ-esque brother were also in attendance.

Though from my understanding the older Sanderson sibling was both elusive and single. Not that either of those things should matter to me, but it was nice to know I wasn't the only one who liked to keep to themselves in this gossip-ridden town.

While Mia and Giselle were practically joined at the hip in their younger years, they were also a few years older than me, which meant when they were giggling over heartthrobs and having sleepovers, I was still playing video games and building Legos.

To be frank, I wasn't part of the *it* crowd, and I didn't spend a lot of time over the Sanderson's. It wasn't even until Giselle's engagement that I'd met her older brother for a millisecond before he was being pulled away by their mother for something.

Still, I had to respect the man for doing his own thing and staying out of the mouths of the Sunday Susans who loved to dish over who was romancing who.

I headed over to the table, if only to say hello and get their orders started, but between the bar and the hightop, something changed.

It was like the closer I got to them, to *him,* I could feel this magnetic pull, like the planets were aligning or some shit.

I shook off the weird feelings as I set my tray down, dispersing the drinks. Mia threw her arms around me, Giselle squealed in excitement, Aaron and Riley entangled in some deep discussion about hockey, and Lane and Lacey were, of course, entranced in one another's eyes as usual.

Which left Julie and Grayson as my focal points.

Heat enveloped me as I caught Grayson's steady gaze, and I couldn't help but meet it.

At the engagement, he'd looked rather dapper in his expensive suit, every bit the well-to-do bachelor, but in the low light of M's Place, dressed down in a pair of tailored chinos and a dark blue button down, his dark hair swept back like some teenage heartthrob from those old magazines, I couldn't help but gape at his features.

His perfect jawline, plush, pouty lips.

Deep, rich hazel eyes that reminded me of autumn sunsets over the lake.

God, he was beautiful.

And like an idiot, I'd only realized I was staring when I heard the tail end of Julie's drink order. I quickly recovered, thankfully, and continued around the table, making eye contact with everyone except the man whose stare was burning a hole in my back at the moment.

Finally, when I could no longer ignore the hot older brother of my sister's bestie, I turned to face him with dignity, but I was weak.

I was barely able to form a coherent sentence around the man, apparently captivated by his dreamy sunset eyes, and the way his shirt clung to his form like a second skin, drawing attention to his toned arms, his strong form.

Somehow, I'd managed to take the man's order without flatlining completely, though I hightailed it back to the bar like I was being chased by fucking zombies, if only to get a breath of air, regain my sanity.

What the hell was wrong with me?

It wasn't like I'd never met or seen the man before, but somehow...

Somehow, this felt different, like we were both meeting again, as someone new.

And I wasn't sure how I felt about that.

Thankfully, Giselle and her party were true to their word. They'd come to let loose, and boy did they let loose.

As I loaded up the empties from their second and third round of drinks, Mia grabbed me by the arm.

"And just where do you think you're going?" she asked with a giggle.

"To the kitchen to drop these off..."

"Play with us," she said as she waved her bingo dabber at me.

"Oh, I don't know if I can, I—"

"Oh come on, Henry, surely you can just tell your boss your unruly customers forced you into it, and the customer is always right," Giselle said with a smirk as she slid a bingo card over to me.

My gaze caught Grayson's, who just shrugged as he drank gracefully from his glass.

"Best not to deny them. They are ruthless," he said, shaking his head to dispel some stray hair that had fallen out of place.

My gaze settled on the way he wrapped his pillowy lips around the large olive, the sight of his tongue along the green skin eliciting my cock to attention.

My mind was apt to wander at the sight, images of those lips wrapped around other things pushed forward in my mind as I wondered what said lips would feel like against mine.

I'd never been a person to deny fantasy, but then again, most of the places I'd worked left little room for attractive men and steamy fantasies to begin with.

GRAYSON

It wasn't like I didn't have a selection here, in Jasper Springs, but I also didn't have the best luck when it came to most things. And I had even worse luck when it came to men. The thought of my ex threatened to rise up, but I shoved it down quickly.

I didn't want to think about the past, and certainly not while I was at work.

While my sister had worked at the same job for the last seven years, I was still looking for that adult career. You know, the one where you get up everyday, punch in, do your thing. The job that might be boring, but was stable.

After getting let go from my last job, I'd had zero luck finding something that paid as well, but I knew waiting tables would be enough to get me by until I'd found something else.

Still, Jasper Springs may have been a lot of things, but it certainly wasn't lacking attractive men who were most certainly out of *my* league.

Grayson slowly sucked the olive, using his teeth to pull it off the toothpick, and I felt my heartbeat quicken. My cock voiced its own opinion by twitching against the inside of my pants, and I was more than thankful my most inappropriate erection was hidden by my damn server apron.

I gulped as I forced myself to break his sensual stare, if only because now was certainly not the time to get all hot and bothered.

"Just one game," Mia pouted.

I sighed, looking over my shoulder at Max, who seemed to be chatting up someone at the bar at the moment, which meant she too was distracted.

Maybe one game wouldn't hurt.

"Sure, but uh, just one game," I said as the host called out the first number, B-6.

I marked it immediately as grunts and yes's surrounded the space. I noticed Grayson had not moved. Instead, he looked rather uninterested in his game.

With every number called, I neared closer to Bingo, eliciting squeals of excitement from my sister and the other party members.

Except Grayson that was, who looked at my card with a scowl.

"G-54!" The host yelled, and my sister yelled "Bingo!" faster than I could comprehend I'd won.

I'd... won!

GRAYSON

Maybe my luck was starting to turn around.

CHAPTER FOUR

Henry

I'D FINALLY BEEN let go close to twelve-thirty. Giselle and her party had already left, and my last table was on their way out. I counted my tips, which did not include my bingo winnings, if only because I didn't feel right claiming them being as I was an employee and on the clock. Instead, I'd let Mia claim them.

She was more excited about the bingo than I was anyway.

"Can you restock the soap in the men's room before you go, Henry?" Max yelled at me over her shoulder as I undid my apron, folding it up and tossing it underneath the bar.

"Yeah, of course," I answered, not even thinking twice about it.

I'd just finished replacing the empty package when I heard the faintest groan from the stall at the end of the men's bathroom.

Panic flooded me because honestly, even though I'd heard stories about the patrons who had a little too much fun, I hadn't had the pleasure of encountering one myself. After all, I'd only been working at M's Place for a couple weeks. Less than a month. I really thought I'd have more time before I had to peel a drunkard off the floor.

I cautiously approached the stall, gently swinging the door in, since it was apparent it wasn't locked. My eyes widened to see Grayson, knees propped up, head leaning against the stall wall, a fresh sheen of sweat on his brow. Despite the fact he looked more than wasted, something about the way his hair was all disheveled, the way he carelessly hung his wrist off his knee, he was still GQ-level hot.

Who looks hot when they are wasted? No one!

"Hey there, Grayson... you, uh... gotta get up, buddy."

Grayson opened one eye, his gaze scanning over me with disdain as a cough escaped his throat.

"I don't have to do shiiiit." He pouted, taking in a deep breath.

I carefully knelt down, getting on his level, forcing him to look at me.

"Bar's closing down, you can't stay here..." I said softly as I pulled out my phone, queuing up Giselle's number.

Grayson's hand stopped me in my tracks as he grabbed mine. My gaze met his and he shook his head.

"Don't... call... my sister."

"I wasn't going to," I lied.

"Bull fucking shit, Henry. This isn't my first fucking rodeo," he growled.

"I was calling you a cab..." I said, switching gears.

Grayson laughed. "I don't need a cab, I have the Porsche."

His sweaty palm against the back of my hand didn't move, and I contemplated what to do.

"You are not driving anywhere under my watch, Grayson."

Grayson scoffed, but he didn't argue.

"You'd look pretty in my baby, baby," he crooned, and I couldn't help but blush. Even if his compliments were the babbles of a drunk man.

"So fucking pretty..."

I could have just left him there, went and got Max and told her he was being a pain in the ass and wouldn't listen. Her tone alone could make a grown man cry and I had no doubt she could whip Grayson into submission easily.

And then I could go home, and Max would take care of everything, and...

But something in the look in Grayson's eyes, amidst the drunken glaze, I saw something else, something that pulled at my own heartstrings.

It was the look I'd had when I felt like I couldn't catch a damn break.

So, I did exactly what I should not do. I slid my phone in my back pocket, and I reached out to help him up.

"Okay, well, this train is leaving in five minutes, so you need get up."

To my surprise, Grayson actually listened to me, rising to his feet. I stood, reaching out to stabilize him, and he fought me off initially.

"I don't need—" Grayson bristled in my

grasp, stumbling in the small space, but I caught him, my reflex almost instantaneous, as if I rescued drunk patrons on the regular.

"I need your keys," I said as I settled my hand around his waist. I half expected him to flinch, but instead he eased up at my touch, relaxing against me as if his body couldn't protest quite the way his mouth did.

"My left pocket," he breathed, and I carefully slid my hand in, my fingers wrapping around the warm metal keyfob.

I took slow, measured steps, if only so he could keep up, garnering a look from Max as we stumbled side by side toward the door.

CHAPTER FIVE

Grayson

THE FAMILIAR WHIRRING of my car door locks sounded in my ears, mingling together with the warmth of Henry's palm against my back. I could feel his heat through the silky fabric, and something about it made me feel relaxed. Relaxed enough that I wanted to curl against said warmth, but I was far too drunk to garner the control I wanted.

I'd fucked up. Royally. That was apparent. I said I'd stop for just one drink, but one turned into two, two turned into three…

It wasn't that I wasn't having a good time, but watching my sister and her fiancé, and even Lacey and Lane—the most annoying couple on the face of the planet—I couldn't help but feel like a fuck up.

Why couldn't I have a boyfriend who was head over heels for me?

Why were the men in my life always too afraid to come clean about who they were or just looking for a fuck around guy?

Why did I always fall for men who would shove me under the bus the first chance they got?

Was I that much of an asshole?

Henry helped ease me into my passenger seat, my head rolling back against the headrest. I groaned as the self-loathing thoughts permeated my brain. His hand slowly slid across my waist as he fastened me in. I couldn't help but stare, with him up so close, noticing the finer features of his perfect, almost innocent looking face. The urge to reach out and run my hand through his dark hair was prevalent, and just as I moved to do so, he pulled away and I dropped my hand. He patted my seatbelt with approval, before shutting my door. It seemed like forever, the moment of pause between his shutting my door, and him getting in the driver's seat, and I half wondered if he had changed his mind, and decided he was going to leave my drunken ass here.

When he folded himself into the driver's seat, I couldn't help but notice the curve of his ass fit nicely, almost as if he was made for it.

As if he was made for me...

I shook the hazy thoughts from my brain, resting my head against the headrest as I closed my eyes, my intoxicated thoughts making themselves known despite my best intentions.

"Do you ever just feel like... like everyone else is on some set path that you don't have access to?" I said, completely not expecting Henry to respond to the words of a drunk asshole like myself.

"Yeah, I, uh... feel like that a lot, actually," he said quietly. For a moment, we just sat there in the silence, and it was... nice.

But my idiotic mouth wanted nothing more than to fill the space.

"It's just, this wedding... it's... it's exhausting." I sighed, opening my eyes. Upon doing so, I noted Henry was staring at me, his hands gripping the steering wheel.

I raised my eyebrow at him in question, noting the blush that crept into his cheeks.

Blushing Henry in the front of my Porsche was not a bad sight.

In fact, it only aided in my inebriated thoughts of fantasy as I imagined myself straddling his lap, my ass backed up against the steering wheel, grinding myself against him. Biting those perfect lips and watching those cheeks pinken from my touch.

My cock twitched its approval of such a situation, but I was also dizzy and did not think I could make the move with enough sophistication at the moment as the room was still spinning.

"I can imagine, being as you're actually in the wedding party," he said.

"That's not... that's not what I meant." I sighed. "It's exhausting having to watch my *younger* sibling get her happy ever after, when I can't have the same thing." I forced myself to look away from the beautiful man in my car, if only because I feared with the uncharacteristic vulnerability I was expelling at the moment, I would fall over the edge and dive into *woe is me* territory.

Poor little rich kid, boo fucking hoo.

I did not *pout* over anything, or anyone for that matter. I was Grayson Sanderson. I was an absolute fucking diamond, and I knew my worth.

Henry spoke up, his voice even and smooth, like hot chocolate.

"I know the feeling. Not because of my sister. I mean, it's like everyone else I know is off getting married and having kids, and buying houses, and I'm just like... I just want a stable job and a boyfriend and like, maybe a cat or something, you know?" Henry said, letting out a sigh.

I turned to look at him, feeling an almost magnet pull, a kindred spirit of sorts. I did know. I knew exactly how it felt to be the black sheep, to be the one off the beaten path. Or maybe it was the several martinis I'd had, making my stomach flip.

Either way, I had the strangest feeling that maybe, just maybe there *was* someone who understood me for once. And that was tempting. Too tempting, to fall into hope.

"You're easy to talk to, you know that?" I said, feeling my heart catch in my throat.

Henry coughed as he broke my gaze, turning on the car.

"We... we should probably get you home," he mumbled as he backed us up, and headed out onto the road.

My shoulders slumped as he looked away, hiding from my words. I got the feeling pretty little Henry didn't get praised enough where it mattered.

Fucking pity.

"You, uh, do you still live at home with your parents, or..."

Shame fell over me immediately at his question, even though it wasn't meant to be derogatory in any way.

My sister had moved out with Aaron pretty much as soon as they'd graduated. I'd moved out too, for a few years, but after mom had hip replacement surgery, I'd moved back to help her out around the house, and just never left. Even though I knew I could anytime, if I wanted.

Maybe I was waiting for the right man to come in and rescue me like a sad princess or something.

God, what is fucking wrong with me?

I meant to say 'yes' like a normal person, but instead all that came out of my mouth was, "I don't have a home," like I was some bridal vagrant.

"Well, how about you stay with me then? For tonight, I mean. It's late, and you can figure out your next move in the morning?" He rushed the words, and I watched his jaw tense while he stared on at the road.

If I didn't know any better, I'd say he was flirting with me, but I knew the truth.

He was just being a Good Samaritan. Any man would have done the same, right?

CHAPTER SIX

Henry

GRAYSON WAS HEAVY against me, but I was no weakling.

Though if lifting trashed patrons becomes a thing, I might have to start going to the gym more.

I fumbled with my keys at the door as he leaned against me, his face pressed against my neck so close I could feel the heat of his breath on my skin. The sudden warmth against my flesh caused goosebumps to rise on my arms, and the way Grayson squeezed my waist, the way he *sighed* when he breathed me in, was a form of intoxication all its own.

What the hell is wrong with me?

I shoved the odd feelings down as I jiggled my key in the lock, the door opening finally, and I squeezed his hips back.

"Come on, big guy, let's get you settled," I huffed as we ambled through the doorway. I flipped the lights on, kicking the back of the door to close it with a soft thud.

"You smell good," he murmured, and I couldn't help but roll my eyes.

"It's not me, it's my Glade Plug-In," I remarked as I led him over to the couch, depositing him there.

He fell with ease against the couch, leaning back against the cushions like he was truly as exhausted as I felt.

He leaned his head back, his lips parting, another sigh leaving him that caused my damn cock to twitch. Without my server apron to hide behind, I silently cursed, thankful he was staring at the ceiling instead of me.

I knelt on the ground, taking my time and easing his shoes off, the leather smooth against my skin. I set them aside, readying to lift his legs onto the couch when I noticed he was staring at me from above, a dark gleam in his eyes that froze me in place.

"Wh... what?" I asked, worried I'd somehow done something wrong, or that this was the moment he was finally going to upchuck.

"You're just... you're fucking beautiful, do you know that?" he said, his words slurred and hazy, but awe-filled nonetheless.

My eyelashes fluttered as I tucked some sweaty, stray strands of hair behind my ear.

I shrugged off his flirtations. After all, he was drunk. Everyone looked pretty with martini goggles.

But in the morning, when he'd see me with my bed head and my Star Wars pajama pants, I doubt he'd think I was beautiful.

I was average, at best, and I was okay with that.

Except at that moment, I wanted to believe his drunken words. I wanted him to see me sober the way he did drunk.

Why, I had no clue, but it didn't change the fact of the matter. Come morning, Grayson wouldn't remember a thing he said tonight.

And he'd go back to his life, and I'd go

back to mine.

"Thanks, but, uh, I think that's your martinis talking. Now, let's get your legs up here," I said as I lifted his legs up one at a time, settling them on the couch cushions, reaching around his waist, if only to situate him so he was elevated enough against my couch pillows that if he did decide to upchuck everywhere, he was less likely to destroy my couch.

And more apt to destroy his shirt.

Which was soft, and warm, and...

Grayson leaned up as I settled him, and I turned to face him. Our faces were just mere inches away, and this close, I couldn't help but notice underneath the scent of gin and olives, he smelled like musk and cedar, hints of orange and pine meddling with the alcohol that was like a hit to my system.

I breathed him in for a moment, appreciating the sight of his dark eyes and lashes, of his perfectly pouty lips.

He leaned closer, his lips hovering just a breath from mine.

I paused only for a moment before turning away. I didn't go around kissing hot, wealthy, intoxicated men. I did have morals, after all, and as badly as I wanted to kiss Grayson—to know if his lips would feel as soft as his shirt—I knew I shouldn't.

But that didn't stop my cock from protesting otherwise.

"Okay... all settled," I whispered as I slid my hands out from underneath him, stepping away. I reached over him, grabbing the blanket that was draped across the back of the couch and quickly unfolding it, covering him in haste. I needed to get as far away from this man as possible, if only to quiet my stupid cock with a mind of its own.

"Henry..." he groaned as I backed away.

"Good night, Grayson," I said, before turning away and running to the safety of my bathroom like a god damned coward.

Only when I was alone, in the sanctity of my bathroom, did I let out a sigh of relief.

I turned on the water for the shower and adjusted the temperature to my liking.

Steam coated my bathroom rather quickly as I disrobed, stepping into the small space and letting the hot water soothe me, washing away the weirdness that had transpired moments ago.

Grayson tried to kiss me.

Because he's drunk, Henry. Not because he's into you.

Bracing myself against the tile, I closed my eyes as I fantasized someone like Grayson could ever be into me.

That *he* could be into me. Images flooded my brain about what he would taste like, the texture of his lips, the salt of his sweat on my tongue.

His swollen cock in my mouth.

Fuck, fuck, fuck, don't go there, Henry.

But it was too late, my cock had already voiced its opinion on the matter, and there was only truly one way to get the thoughts to leave. I groaned in guilt as I wrapped my hand around my shaft, the friction a most satisfying sensation. I leaned into my hold, slowly rocking my hips forward, building a rhythm. My palm was wet and warm, and the slide of my cock against it elicited a deep groan out of me.

I wondered about those perfect, pouty lips of his, and what it would feel like to press my mouth to his, what his mouth would feel like along my skin, biting and sucking my flesh at all my sweet spots.

Beneath my ear, on my neck.

And most certainly, I wondered what his lips would feel like wrapped around my cock, his tongue licking me clean of the precum that was currently coating my hand and shaft.

I thought about that dark look he'd given me as I knelt before him, my hands around his ankles.

I fantasized about him *commanding* me to *take care of him.*

I came without warning, grunting in guilt and relief, leaning my head against the tile, watching the ropes of my release circle the drain, round and round.

My breathing started to even out as I tugged the last remainders of my release out of my softening cock, and I knew I needed to put Grayson Sanderson as far out of my mind as possible.

Because this... this wasn't some romance novel.

This was life, and the truth was that aside from Giselle's wedding, I'd probably never see Grayson again.

Right?

I finished cleaning myself, turned off the water, and climbed out. Wrapping a fluffy towel around my waist, I used another to quickly dry my hair. I grabbed a clean pair of sleep pants and slipped them up my legs, pulling a t-shirt on over my head.

Finally dressed, I slipped out of my bathroom to check on Grayson before heading to bed myself, noting that he was passed out, snoring away. I noticed however, the blanket I'd given him had fallen to the ground and he was now sleeping on his side.

I sauntered over quietly, doing my best as to not make a peep and wake him. Slowly, I knelt to pick the blanket up, carefully laying it over him. I gently tucked it in the back, taking a moment to appreciate the beauty of his slumber, like a freaking weirdo.

He looked so peaceful, so content. It was envious.

"Good night, Grayson," I whispered, even though I knew he couldn't hear me.

And when I said good night to him, I promised myself that it would end there.

The fantasy, the hope.

Come morning, everything would go back to normal, the way it was supposed to be.

I slipped into my bedroom, beneath my

sheets, and let my own wave of exhaustion take me under.

And I dreamed of wild, amber eyes, and pouty lips, and wedding bells in a forest full of pine.

CHAPTER SEVEN

Henry

THE SOUND OF clanging and crashing stirred me from my sleep. For a moment, I panicked until I realized exactly what was the cause of the crashing. Or rather who.

I rubbed my eyes, and scraped my fingernails over my scruff, slowly ambling through my hallway to the kitchen. Sure enough, I found Grayson opening and closing cabinets, my kitchen in a little bit of disarray, but not as disheveled as the man in front of me.

His shirtsleeves were rolled up, and his hair was a bit messy, no doubt from sleeping on the square pillows.

"What are you doing?" I inquired, my voice still slightly groggy from my abrupt awakening.

Grayson stopped his tirade, turning to me slowly, eyes appraising me as if *I* was the one who was daft.

"I can not find any espresso in this god forsaken place," he said with poise, shaking his head as if it were quite obvious. "This house needs, espresso. I need—"

I casually opened the cabinet nearest to me, the slender one that didn't fit much in it other than drink mixes and of course, coffee. I grabbed the brown paper bag of freshly ground morning roast that I'd purchased a few days ago.

I could feel Grayson's eyes on me like a hawk. I casually set the bag down in front of him on the counter, meeting his gaze.

"What is this?" he asked, though he didn't look at the coffee. Instead, his gaze was fixed on me, on my lips. I couldn't help but smirk up at the towering man.

"Espresso." I deadpanned.

"This—" Grayson said as he took the bag from my hands, opening it to sniff it and frowning. "This is *store bought* coffee."

"Caffeine is caffeine, either you want it or—" I remarked as I snatched the bag back, heading over to the coffee machine.

"I suppose in a pinch, it will do." Grayson mewled, almost as if I'd caused him a great deal of trauma by offering him a fresh, hot cup of coffee.

It didn't take long for me to throw a pot together, and I continued on my morning routine, opening the fridge and gathering my supplies for breakfast. Eggs, bacon, bread...

"Do not feel as if you have to do this on my behalf," Grayson said as I set the ingredients down, setting up my skillet and turning the burner on. I tossed some bacon in, letting it sizzle.

"Aren't you hungover? Hungry?" I asked as I cracked the eggs into a second pan.

Grayson casually leaned against my island, crossing his arms. I could feel his gaze on me like a laser beam; hot, holding me in place.

"Please, I am not some amateur, Henry. I am a professional. I do not get *hungover*. Not anymore."

"I don't think that is the selling point you seem to think it is," I said, realizing I sounded kind of like an asshole. I usually wasn't so loose lipped around people, but Grayson didn't feel like most people. It was far too easy to just say what was on my mind around him, and that was dangerous.

The last thing I wanted to do was piss him off, even if it was only because I didn't want him running to his sister and complaining, and for the wedding itself to be awkward because I had slipped up and said something stupid.

"Yes, well, my *selling points* have not been a problem for most people," he bit out, like a bratty child.

I don't know why, but his attitude made my cock twitch, and a grin erupt on my face.

Maybe I need the coffee more than he does.

I turned the bacon once more as the coffee pot beeped. Naturally, I took my time, grabbing some mugs and setting them down, pouring the coffee while breakfast cooked.

"Cream?" I asked as I opened the fridge once more to grab my french vanilla store brand creamer.

"Fuck..." I heard him curse, and I

turned to look at him as he ran his hand over his face, shaking his head.

Maybe he still felt off from last night...

"You okay?" I asked as I set the bottle down.

Grayson nodded. "Yes, I'm fine, I just..."

"What, Jasper Springs Market ain't good enough for you?" I asked, raising my eyebrow.

Why the fuck did I just say that?

I never was this brash, this upfront with anyone!

Grayson flipped some dark hair out of his eyes, the motion drawing attention to his slender neck, his perfectly sinuous shoulders, his toned, pale arms.

"I mean... yes. To the cream. And two sugar cubes," he said poignantly.

I couldn't help but laugh as I opened the slender cabinet yet again, pulling out two slim cane sugar packets.

"Well, hopefully this will be good enough. I call it 'deconstructed sugar cube'," I said, flashing him a smirk as I passed him the packets.

He took them out of my fingers, his long ones brushing mine in transfer. His touch was soft, warm, and I liked it.

Stupidly, I wished I could hold onto it a little longer, but I knew I needed to put all those thoughts—about him, about me, and whatever weird tension had somehow built between us—out of my brain.

I hurriedly finished up with the coffee, sliding him his mug as I manned the stove. I tossed the bread in the toaster oven, and for a moment with everything going, I paused to take a sip of my coffee, noticing once again Grayson was staring at me.

"I should go," he said, though he made no move to set down his mug. In fact, his hand gripped it tighter, and I could see the steam wafting in the air, contrasted by his shirt.

"You should eat something first. Can't let you go on an empty stomach, after all."

"If you insist," he said, straightening his posture as if he was challenging me to a dual or something.

I gripped my own coffee, letting the warmth spread from my fingertips.

The toast popped up, breaking the odd tension, and I set my coffee down, gesturing for my guest to sit at the island, amidst the mess he'd made as he tore everything out of my cupboards looking for his beloved *espresso.*

"Order up," I said as I plated his food.

Something passed between us as I stood beside him, only inches away. I set his plate in front of him, but his gaze held me still like I was truly the prey, and he was a vicious hunter.

My cock stood at attention, liking the heat of being on the spot as he pinned me there with his dark, amber gaze.

Bad idea, Henry.

Bad, bad fucking idea.

Just walk away now and no one gets hurt.

Especially you.

I swallowed harshly as I backed away, if only to break the spell that had formed between us. Maybe Grayson wasn't the only one hungover.

Hungover on pretty rich boys who smell like heaven and look like a goddamn wet dream sitting in my kitchen.

"Thanks," he said as I slid him a fork, going about to fixing my own meal.

We ate in silence. Awkward, charged silence. Thankfully, Grayson ate his breakfast and sucked down his coffee rather quickly, and before I'd even finished my own cup of coffee, he was walking toward the door.

"Well, this has been lovely and all, Henry, but I believe I have overstayed my welcome," he said.

"Grayson, wait..." I said, feeling a bit like an asshole. I didn't want him to stay, but I also didn't want him to leave.

Grayson stopped just before the door, as I caught up to him.

"I just... don't want things to be weird... between us," I said, trying to articulate something I barely understood at the time.

He narrowed his gaze at me, furrowing his eyebrows. "Why would anything be weird?" he asked.

I closed my eyes, realizing how stupid I must have looked. I'd assumed maybe, just maybe, he remembered an inkling of what had happened, how he'd tried to kiss me, but assuming from his reaction, he didn't.

Or he did, and he just didn't care. Either way, I knew I was obsessing, and I just needed to let it go. I needed to let him go.

"Oh, uh, nothing, I just..." I sighed, giving up as I opened the door. "Do you need a ride?"

GRAYSON

Grayson held up his car keys. "You drove my car here, remember? As I said, I have overstayed my welcome. You have been most hospitable, but I will not burden you further," he said with a slight, polite smile.

I nodded in understanding. "Oh, yes, of course. Okay."

I'd be lying if I said it didn't bother me. A part of me, a sad, lonely part had actually wanted the excuse to drive him back, if only because for some reason, I liked being around the man.

Not to mention his leaving would mean the momentary excitement would dissipate, and I'd be back to my normal, boring life.

Punch in, punch out.

Go home, alone.

Maybe I really do need to get out more.

I held the door open for him and he stepped through, stopping halfway. The motion put us rather close together, close enough when he turned to me, I could see the flecks of gold in his amber eyes. Feel his hot, bacon-scented breath on my face.

Instinctively, I leaned in closer, almost as if pulled by an invisible force. Like he was too hard to resist, and I knew I should.

"Goodbye, Grayson," I said, my voice a dark, breathy whisper. My gaze fell from his sunset eyes to his pillowy, pouty lips.

"Goodbye, Henry," he whispered, his tongue darting out to lick his lips in a motion that made my damn cock throb.

Think unsexy thoughts, Henry.

And with that he just... left.

He left me standing halfway in the hall of my apartment complex, hot, hard, and wanting.

Some people in this life are just lucky, people like Grayson.

But I wasn't a lucky boy.

I would never have the things I wanted, because what I wanted was well beyond my means, beyond my pay grade, beyond my reach.

And as I cleaned up the mess Grayson had left, I vowed to put him and all thoughts of him to rest, once and for all, for the sake of my own sanity.

CHAPTER EIGHT

Grayson

I SIGHED AS the incessant beeping from my phone echoed in the empty air of my humble abode.

I wasn't usually home at this hour of the day, but the corporate gods had decided to grace me with a three days off in a row this week.

I was still skeptical if Caroline and Sven would be able to hold down *Shimmer*, the bridal boutique I'd been working at for the last ten years.

Truthfully, I loved my job, I really did. I enjoyed every aspect of previewing the dresses and the wedding pantsuits too. I enjoyed styling women from all walks of life, and watching them completely come undone when they set their eyes on *the one*. When they saw themselves for the first time in that perfect gown, when they realized everything they knew was going to change.

Hell, I even loved dealing with the drama behind the desk, and gossiping with my co-workers. I knew how to manage *Shimmer*. What I didn't know how to do, apparently, was manage my fucking life.

I still couldn't believe I'd been such a lush the night prior, and not only that, I'd made a gigantic fool of myself in front of Henry, which shouldn't have bothered me as much as it did.

For some reason I cared what he thought. But thankfully, another rampant *ding* pulled me from my pity party, and I prepared to gloat in all my glory, expecting Caroline to message me with sad emojis because she was utterly incapable of running the show without someone telling her what to do.

And Sven is about as useful as a bag of rocks.

Very pretty rocks, but I digress...

Only, when I opened my notifications, I

saw it wasn't my ill-fated co-workers who were messaging me with pleas to save them. It was my sister.

Honestly, I still don't know which would have been worse.

I sighed indignantly, knowing it was best to respond to her.

Apologies, I was out and only just got back. What's up?

Giselle tapped away quickly, sending me the eyeballs emoji.

And where were you at the tender hour of 9am on your day off?

A part of me debated lying to her, but I also knew better than to try and keep anything from my sister. She could smell a fib a mile away, even through text. So I shrugged, bit my lip and just let the cat out of the bag. It was better that way, at least then I could control the narrative.

If you must know, the martinis landed me on Henry's couch last night.

I waited for the onslaught of her words, and sure enough, she fired them off without haste.

You what? I thought you had a ride... you said... wait, you didn't...

I rolled my eyes.

Please, I'm not that easy, Giselle!

I texted her back. *I did nothing of the sort, and Henry was a complete gentlemen. A perfect prince charming. Drove me home and put me up for the night.*

I paused, wanting to say more, which was odd.

I never really felt the desire to spill *all* my secrets and feelings to my sister. Usually, I only gave her the bare minimum of information, but it seemed after Henry's home cooked breakfast... and the close proximity against his door... I was feeling uncharacteristically off. Maybe I was still drunk.

Well, hopefully you won't be too hungover to join Aaron and I for dinner tonight.

I fell back against the couch, the cushions squeaking. The memory of Henry's soft couch cradling me threatened to erupt in my brain, but I pushed it away.

Now was not the time to grieve over such things.

Just you and Aaron? I asked, twisting my lips in suspicion.

Every Sunday, up until Mom had her surgery, rain or shine, we had family dinner. And even if I didn't want to admit it, when I was living on my own, it was always nice to come home at least once a week and catch up with my sister, and devour my mom's delectable desserts.

But those dinners were a thing of the past now, and my sister seemed to want to pick up the torch, which shouldn't have bothered me, but...

Being over at Giselle's was like stepping into the world I wanted, but knew I couldn't have. And as much as I was proud of my sister for all she'd accomplished, and the life she and her groom-to-be had built, if my parents were in the room, I'd never hear the end of it.

The tiny little digs at my job, at my perpetual singleness, my perpetual failure to launch.

Mom and Dad are coming too, duh.

I leaned my head back on the couch cushion, debating how to answer. It wasn't like I didn't see enough of them already, but going over for dinner was a level of self-inflicted trauma I wasn't sure I was up for at the moment.

My sister must have taken my pause for urgency, because she tapped out two texts in rapid succession.

Please, Grayson... it would mean a lot to me to have all of you here.

It'll be just like old times, I promise.

Leave it to my sister to lay on the dramatics. Maybe it was her pleading, maybe it was because for a moment I dared to hope it *could* be like the good old days.

Before I'd embarrassed myself and my family.

Before I knew I'd be alone forever.

I'll have to get back to you a little later. I'm in desperate need of a shower right now.

It was a shitty response, but I was getting too close for comfort. And I really *did* need a shower.

I meant what I said to Henry. His hospitality was more than spent, and I didn't expect to start showering at his place and walking around it like I lived there or something. No, as far as I was concerned, he'd done his part, and I needed to take care of myself.

But I'd be lying if I said that I didn't find some sort of twisted satisfaction in the way he took my shoes off, the way he covered me, making sure I was comfortable.

The way he *took care* of me.

The memories flooded me, hazy as I remembered how close he'd been to me. The heat from his breath warmed my skin, and his lips looked so deliciously plump, the desire to suck on them, to kiss them was like a living breathing entity all its own.

And for a moment, he looked at me with the same hunger, the same desire, and I leaned in just a fraction...

Fucking hell.

I peeled myself off the couch. Maybe my sister was right; maybe I was that easy. Pump me full of a few drinks and I'll fall to my knees for prince charming.

But there wouldn't be any falling on any knees. Not now, and certainly not in my future since I'd probably fucked that up too.

I waltzed through the quiet house, until I'd come to my bathroom, relishing in the privacy. My father was religious about his job—I guess the apple didn't fall far from the tree there—and my mother spent most of her days volunteering at the local Jasper Springs Library.

Until four thirty, I had the Sanderson estate all to myself.

Sliding into the shower as the hot steam filled the room was a welcome relief.

Instantly, I let out a groan, letting the water rush over my chilled skin.

My memory was hazy at best, but I could still remember that look Henry gave me, the way his gaze fell to my lips, how his Adam's apple bobbed just before he'd parted his lips.

Before he'd walked away.

My cock stood at attention almost immediately upon his memory, and I sighed in defeat.

That wasn't what I came here for.

But I was alone, and I was hot, and I knew the release would feel good. And after the night—and awkward morning—I'd had, I wanted to feel better.

So, I closed my eyes as I wrapped my hand around my cock, slowly stroking my shaft as I let my mind wander.

I let Henry's image fill my brain, of him on his knees before me, hands undressing me. Only this time in my vision, he didn't stop at my shoes. This time he painstakingly took his time, unlatching my belt, unzipping my pants...

Fuck.

My cock twitched at the thought of Henry and his long fingers playing at the buttons of my chinos, unzipping me.

Wrapping said fingers around my swollen, leaking head.

A deep, unrelenting grunt escaped my throat and I snapped my hips, picking up more rhythm, thrusting my cock faster into my fist, as I let my fantasies take flight.

I imagined his fingertips brushing over my slit, gathering my wetness before sliding those pretty fingers into his perfect mouth, where I could watch him lick and suck my precum off his coated digits.

And then I imagined kissing him, letting my tongue roll over his, biting, sucking at his bottom lip like a goddamned lollipop until I could taste myself. I imagined his wet cock sliding against my own, hard and slick, erupting over the both of us.

I nearly slid against the tile as my orgasm pushed forth, the sound of ecstasy leaving my throat a strained, deep sound that was somewhere between a moan and a plea for mercy.

My cock pulsed, throbbing as I came and I tried to catch my breath.

It felt like forever until I'd gone soft, until I'd come back down from whatever dimension my astronomical orgasm had taken me to. Water ran down my face, down my arms and chest, washing away my fantasies like the sins they truly were.

CHAPTER NINE

Grayson

WHEN I'D DRESSED in clean clothes, I felt a fraction better, but there was still the matter of my stomach. While Henry's impromptu breakfast had been good, it was nearing noon. I checked my pockets of my clothes from the previous night, expecting to find my wallet, but it was not there. Panic flooded me as I retraced my steps, trying to remember where I'd put it or if I'd left it in my car.

It seemed to be missing from my house entirely. It wasn't in the kitchen, or the bathroom or... I rushed outside and pulled open the car door, a quick check of my glovebox revealed that was certainly not the case. I trudged back inside, pressing my fingers to the bridge of my nose as I tried to force the memories to reveal where I'd left the damn thing.

My eyelashes fluttered as reality rushed over me, because I knew it would cost me—in ways that had nothing to do with my wallet.

Because the truth was, the likeliest of places my wallet probably was, was at Henry's house.

But I couldn't just show up at his house hours after leaving like some crazy motherfucker. That would be far too stalker-ish.

So instead, I pulled up my text, and sent my sister a text.

Do you happen to have Henry's number?

True to her nature, my sister let me stew a moment before answering, which only meant this truly was going to be a bargain.

I do... But why do you need it?

I cursed as I tapped out my response, knowing full well I was at her mercy.

Because I think I may have accidentally left my wallet at his house.

Giselle texted me a string of judgmental emojis, complete with a kissy face.

I think someone is smitten.

I sighed in repose.

It's not like that. It's just an honest mistake, and I'd like to get it back.

A string of emojis burst on my screen, followed by her response.

I mean, that's like the oldest play in the book, Gray.

She wasn't wrong, it was rather cliché, but it wasn't like I'd *planned* to do such things. I could scheme just as good as anyone else, but I'd never stoop to such basic ploys to land a man. I had other charms for that.

Sure enough though, my words did not dissuade her from wheeling and dealing.

I'll give it to you if you promise to come to dinner tonight.

I grit my teeth, but I knew I would say yes. Especially if I wanted my wallet back.

Fine.

And when she sent over his number in a flash, I knew my fate was sealed.

CHAPTER TEN

Henry

THE LAST THING I expected to get during my day of adulting was a text from Grayson. For starters, I'd never given him my number, but that didn't mean it wasn't accessible.

A part of me dared to get my hopes up, thinking maybe, just maybe...

But my thoughts were quickly shut down when I realized he'd messaged me because he'd left his wallet at my house.

Of course.

I finished putting my groceries away, and headed over to the couch, sliding my hand behind the cushions, and sure enough... a hard, smooth bulky object met my palm. Wrapping my fingers around it, I pulled it out. The Italian leather was cool to the touch.

My timer on my phone went off, telling me I needed to get my ass moving if I wanted to make it to the cafe to grab lunch before my shift started.

Are you able to meet me at Jasper Springs Cafe?

I slid his wallet in my pocket as I set about to grab my keys and head out the door. I'd just made it to the car when he answered.

When?

I texted back quickly.

How about twenty minutes?

His response came just as fast.

Yes, that would be great.

I tossed my phone in the cup holder, turning on the radio with an exaggerated sigh. For some reason, my nerves were getting the best of me. It wasn't like it was a date or anything. I mean, the guy was literally just coming to retrieve his wallet. But there was a part of me—a hopeful, wishful part—that dared to think maybe it could be more. Maybe... just maybe, we could grab a coffee and have lunch like two normal friends.

GRAYSON

Friend.

I didn't like the taste of that word on my tongue, but Grayson wasn't really an acquaintance either.

I shoved the thoughts down as I drove off for the cafe. Maybe I was just having an off day because of everything that had transpired last night, or that weird tension that had formed between us this morning on my doorstep.

Whatever the case was, I needed to focus on the task at hand. Lunch, wallet delivery, and making it to work on time.

CHAPTER ELEVEN

Henry

THE CAFE ITSELF was bustling at this hour, since it was the preferred lunch stop for most of the nine to fivers due to the fact that they had phenomenal sandwiches, as well as their delicious bottomless coffee. Not to mention they were *fast*.

I noticed him first, leaning languidly against the windowpane. I paused for a moment, taking in the sight of him. He couldn't see me from where he was standing inside, my small Toyota hidden by the oversized SUV in front of me, which gave me the guiltiest feeling. Like I was being a total creeper, but I couldn't help it.

With the light pouring in, lighting up his dark hair and features, in his business casual slacks and button down...

He looked positively dreamy.

Snap out of it, Henry!

I sighed as I headed toward the cafe, my stomach growling with a hunger that went far beyond food.

The bell jingled as I opened the door, and was assaulted with the incredible scent of fresh, percolating coffee and garlic bread. I sucked in a deep breath of the wonderful aromas and headed over to Grayson with quickening strides.

"Hey," I said nervously, causing him to look up from his phone. His dark gaze settled on me, the corners of his lips turning up in a polished, genuine smile.

"Hey," he said, flashing me with a smile.

Sweat had already started to bead on my skin and my stomach decided to protest its indignities at that moment, turning his precious smile into a frown.

"You, uh... want to get something to eat?" he asked awkwardly.

"I mean, I'm sure you have a busy schedule, so we should probably just—"

"Tell you what, you give me my wallet and I'll buy you lunch. It's the least I can do after acting like a fucking asshole last night."

His words settled on me, and I wasn't sure how to feel about his offer. In my experience, people usually weren't just... nice out of the kindness of their hearts. At least not to me, anyway.

But I never let that stop me from being who I was. From helping people or giving parts of myself away.

Though what I had to offer a man like Grayson was beyond me, I still couldn't begrudge him for trying to make amends, even if it was just because he felt guilty.

What kind of man would I be if I denied him the chance to placate his well-groomed conscience?

I slid my hand in my back pocket, if only to make sure I still had his wallet, the whole reason for the meeting, after all, which I did.

"I mean, that's not really necessary..." I said as I handed him his wallet.

Grayson took it from me, his fingers brushing the backs of mine. The smooth, warm feel of his skin against mine sent a jolt through me, fueling my goblin brain once more as I wondered involuntarily what his body would feel like against my own.

Naked.

Before I could even stop myself, my cock sprang to life, and I pulled away.

"I insist," he said as he waved me toward the line of people at the register.

Caught between a rock and a literal hard place, I didn't want to be rude.

But I was also acutely aware of my current situation, and didn't want to upset the already delicate balance between Grayson and I.

And I really *was* hungry.

Damn it.

"Fine," I said, as I all but raced him to the line, keeping my sights trained on the menu if only to try and focus on unsexy thoughts.

Grayson came up behind me, and I could feel his warmth. My overactive imagination immediately wanted to dive off the deep end into more highly inappropriate thoughts, and it truly was a struggle to remain vigilant.

Fuck me sideways...

Just as the line moved, I did too, deciding I'd keep my order simple. Just a coffee and a smoked gouda and ham panini. It was my usual order.

"That's it?" Grayson raised an eyebrow at me.

I shrugged, not wanting to appear as judged as I felt.

What's wrong with a coffee and a panini?

"I like to keep it simple," I said, feeling on the spot.

Grayson nibbled his lips, his gaze darting from me to the cashier. "I'll have a prosciutto caprese melt with a bowl of tomato bisque and one oversized cinnamon roll."

Judging from Grayson's stature and shape, I truly wondered where the hell he was going to put all that food. I wasn't the most in shape man in the world, but I would have bet my bingo winnings he was one of those health-food nuts who spent a lot of time at the gym

"Something simple, and sweet. To say thanks," he said, flashing me with a smirk that only made my insides rush with warmth, and my cock spring back to life.

Save me now!

It would appear that my prayers would be answered, as that was the moment my sister texted me, the loud and obnoxious ringtone going off like a siren in the otherwise cozy and quaint cafe. Grayson chuckled as I snuck away to the counter to retrieve my *simple* order, while he paid.

I hurriedly silenced the text, noticing some of the looks from other patrons who must've been utterly disturbed by the loud screeching Stewie from Family Guy sound that played every time she messaged me.

Once I'd settled myself down in a seat and set my tray down, I pulled out my phone, hiding my own embarrassment behind the lights of my bright display.

Did you get your schedule yet?

I stare at my sister's text, debating if I should answer. Technically, I wouldn't get the schedule until I went into work, but she didn't know that.

I could very easily just tell her I wasn't available for the weekend trip she'd been *begging* to come on with Giselle and the rest of the party.

As if he could read my mind, Grayson sat down with his tray of food, his smooth voice penetrating my thoughts.

"You look like you've seen a ghost," Grayson said, and he took a sip of his coffee, crossing his long legs.

I looked up from my phone at the fine specimen in front of me, and for some strange reason, I divulged the truth.

I seemed to do that a lot around Grayson. Drunk or not.

"It's my sister, she's... been up my ass about this damn Wine Fest trip coming up."

"Giselle's trip?" he asked, looking slightly confused.

I nodded in response.

"I wasn't aware you were invited to that," he said, and I couldn't deny the words bit. I knew he wasn't trying to be rude, but his shock at the admission only cemented my suspicion that I just wouldn't fit in.

"Well, it's not like I'm going or anything," I said defensively. "Lord knows, I wouldn't fit in with all of you yuppies anyway." The words fell out of my mouth before I could stop them.

Grayson's eyebrows furrowed, and he had the audacity to look *hurt*.

Like I was the asshole.

Maybe I was. Maybe that was my curse

in life—to be a grumpy, lonely old asshole struggling to find his happy ever after because everyone and everything was too good for him.

"I see," was all he said, as he picked up his tray. "I just remembered, I have a meeting in about fifteen minutes. Guess I'm getting this to go," he said, and my heart splintered.

I would have bet my last dollar there was no meeting, and I'd just single-handedly detonated the one chance I might have had.

Stupid, Henry!

Fuck!

I watched as he gracefully approached the counter, as the employees packaged his sandwich, and as he walked out the door without so much as looking at me or waving goodbye.

And suddenly I wasn't so hungry anymore.

CHAPTER TWELVE

Henry

ALL DAY I'D stared at my phone. At the conversation I'd started with Grayson. Our meeting at the cafe was gnawing at me.

I hadn't meant my words to sound so harsh, but perhaps there was some truth to them. It was probably apparent to anyone with eyeballs that we were in stark contrast. While my sister and I had both grown up in the same house, with the same parents, she'd always been starstruck by the finer things in life. It was her mission to be *one of them,* and being besties with Giselle exposed her to such things. Gave her opportunities purely because she'd aligned herself with the upper echelon.

Though to be clear, she wasn't some wealth-chaser who was happy to lap up scraps or anything. She fit in that world just as much as Giselle and her brother did.

Everyone in Giselle's circle was like her. They had everything.

Love, money, nice houses, good jobs.

A weekend in the mountains "glamping" with my sister and her preppy friends, sniffing wine I couldn't pronounce, did not sound ideal to me.

But maybe that was the point.

Maybe I needed to leave my comfort zone and put myself out there.

I hovered my thumb over the screen on my phone for only a moment before my co-worker, Andi, passed me, jostling me from my trance.

"Cara just sat your table five," she said as she started throwing a side salad together.

I sighed, shoving the phone back in my apron pocket. "Thanks," I murmured, exiting the kitchen and strolling over to the table.

GRAYSON

But the moment I left those doors and set my gaze on my table, I wanted to run right back.

Because sitting alone, looking like a goddamn snack of revenge, was fucking Grayson Sanderson.

Well, better get this humiliation over with.

"Can I, uh... get you something to drink?" I said as I forced myself to stand tall, look him in his deep amber eyes, and act as if I hadn't just completely made an ass out of myself earlier.

To my surprise, Grayson only looked at me with a gaze that was a mix of dark and inviting, and apathetic.

"Fancy meeting you here. Again," he said.

I crossed my arms involuntarily as I regaled him. "Well, this *is* my place of business. But you already knew that."

God what was wrong with me?

Why do I just have to worst fucking word vomit around this man?

It's like he's a curse or something!

Grayson twisted his perfect pout, shrugging. "Perhaps I just needed a drink after a long day."

I sighed in defeat. "Let me guess, gin

martini with extra olives?”

Grayson smirked, a dark chuckle escaping his lips.

“Heavens, no. I wouldn't want this to turn into an episode of Groundhog Day.”

I actually laughed.

Like an idiot.

“Well then, what it'll be, *Grayson?*”

“Perhaps I shall keep it simple with a rum and coke.”

“Noted,” I said as I slowly backed away, making my way to the bar.

“Whattaya need, Henry?” Max asked as she wiped the bar down again. She was meticulous about constantly wiping it down and I wasn't entirely sure it wasn't out of boredom and not some undiagnosed OCD.

“Rum and coke.” I said, taking a moment to breathe.

She looked from me to Grayson before raising an eyebrow. “Isn't that the guy you escorted home last night?” she asked with a grin.

“It's not what you think, I promise.”

Max laughed. “Better not be. I ain't running an escort service, sweetheart.”

I rolled my eyes. “Besides, I already put my foot in my mouth,” I murmured as she slid me the drink.

"Too bad, so sad. Hey, those days you put in for, you got 'em."

My blood chilled.

"I... what?" I wasn't entirely sure I heard her correctly, and my panic button was already at an all-time high.

Max cleared her throat, obviously taking my shock as I didn't *hear* her. And instead she all but *yelled*, "Those days for the big wedding trip this weekend. You got 'em. Go spend the weekend with your friends and make sure you have a glass on me!"

My cheeks flushed and I hurriedly grabbed Grayson's drink, caught between the devil and the deep blue sea.

I all but threw his drink at him because I was so agitated over everything that happened.

It truly was the worst fucking day ever.

"Should probably tell your boss you're not spending your time with a bunch of yuppies," he drawled as he took a sip. "I thought about mentioning it to your sister, but..."

I huffed indignantly. "Are you legit blackmailing me into going on a trip?" I asked, my neck aching from all the whiplash.

I watched as he sipped his drink, his lips shimmering with fresh moisture from the alcohol.

Lips that looked far too tempting...

No, Henry!

I watched as he slid his hand in his pocket, pulling his phone out, and I panicked.

Sue me.

I lunged for his phone, not needing him to tattle on me like a grade-schooler to my sister of all people, my stupid, senseless jabberings.

The motion pushed his chair back, pitching me into his lap haphazardly, our faces only inches from one another. He gazed down at me, raising an eyebrow, his smirk more than amused.

Up close like this, the heat between us was undeniable. I should have known then that I would be a goner when it came to Grayson. The man knew just how to press my buttons.

I fought to regain my composure, knowing there were multiple eyes on us. Including Maxine's.

"Do not say a word about this... to my sister."

GRAYSON

"Or what? Hmmm? What will you do, Henry?" He grinned, and I realized he liked this.

He liked playing with me and my emotions.

Because he truly was an asshole.

And I was at a disadvantage, and he knew that.

"Giselle and Mia will be so happy to hear you are coming," he taunted as I righted myself, brushing off my apron with a huff.

The prevalent *need*, the desire, to do as this man said was like someone had lobotomized me.

I'd never wanted to *obey* someone's demands—albeit outlandish demands—so badly.

Maybe there really was something wrong with me.

As I delved into a spiral of madness, Grayson spoke.

"Someone really should mop up that spill," he hollered over me at Maxine. "Poor old Henry could have been sorely injured," he said with a wicked grin.

Abruptly, I turned away, leaving a chuckling, smug Grayson in my wake.

What had I gotten myself into?

CHAPTER THIRTEEN

Grayson

I SWEAR THE Kardashians had nothing on the Sanderson's. Because as I sat in my sister's dining room at her table, next to my mother and across from my sister and father, I was about ready to lose my shit.

It seemed the sole rum and coke I'd had to loosen up my tense nerves had not been enough. Because I'd barely been at her humble abode for an hour before our mother launched into her alcohol-infused interrogation.

As if living under the same roof wasn't enough turmoil.

You can leave at any time, Gray.

But I was truly a glutton for punishment, it seemed.

And running away to the kitchen hadn't been enough of a clue that I didn't wish to have the conversation.

"All I'm saying, is you're pushing forty, Grayson. You should be settling down, laying roots, not—"

I set about to fixing a drink, a martini. Perhaps I could drown myself in olives and gin and none of their words would hit me.

"I'm perfectly content with my life the way it is," I lied.

My father—a man with the utmost impeccable timing—must have had nothing better to do, because as soon as I'd poured the liquid, a waft of cigar smoke poured into the room.

"Your mother has a point, Gray. How can you sell happily ever after if you don't subscribe to the newsletter yourself?"

I shook my head as I gripped the glass tightly. My gaze settled on my sister, who was leaning against the entrance to the kitchen, her eyebrows furrowed.

She mouthed, "Sorry."

Yeah, I bet she was sorry. Sorry that our family drama ruined her prize pot roast dinner.

Not sorry that she'd suckered me into the seventh circle of hell dressed up like Martha Stewart.

"I don't need to be a delusional romantic to have a sense of purpose, but I don't suppose you would know anything about purpose considering your own commitments," I drawled.

"What the hell is that supposed to mean?" he said as he narrowed his eyes at me.

"Nothing," I said as I all but shot back my drink.

"Perhaps you should go easy on that, Gray," my mother said, hiccupping from her own round of liquid courage.

The same liquid courage that spurred her to bring up my skeletons in the first place.

I pulled the shaker from her, turning my back.

"I only learned from the best, mother. Isn't this how one is supposed to deal with meddling, pain in the ass family?" I shot my father a look, raising my eyebrow at him. His jaw tensed, but he didn't say anything. Instead, he only puffed on his cigar like an angry old man.

"Gray..." my sister called out, but I'd had enough.

I stormed through the kitchen door, out to the covered deck, traipsing over to the fire pit Aaron was lighting.

The door slammed shut, and within seconds, I heard my sister's voice.

"Aaron, baby, can you give us a minute," she said softly.

Aaron looked between us, then at the shaker in my hand. He shrugged, kissing his fiancé on the cheek as he headed indoors. "Whatever you say, sweetheart."

When the door slammed once more, I knew we were truly alone.

"Have they sent in reinforcements?" I said as I popped the top off the shaker. I hadn't even bothered to pour it in a glass.

What was the point?

Giselle took a seat next to me, setting her hand on my thigh. "They just want to see you happy, Gray."

"I am happy!" I yelled, but Giselle did not flinch.

"I think we both know you're not. You're afraid."

I scoffed at her.

How dare she!

"I am not afraid of mom and dad..."

"Afraid of change, I mean," she said.

I didn't like the way her words made me feel, so instead, I ignored her, focusing on my drink left in the shaker instead. "Change is inevitable," I murmured.

"It is. And it's a good thing, you know."

I looked at her with softness, her round face, her pristine eyes. She'd always been such a positive ray of sunshine, a believer in the most whimsical of things.

The exact opposite of me.

My parent's words reverberated in my head, acting as if my age was some expiration date, and if I didn't lock a man down in the next two years, I would be an old maid.

Or an old butler, technically.

"It's okay to not be okay, Gray. It doesn't make you a failure."

"Is that what your therapist tells you, sweetheart?" I asked, and the minute I said it I regretted it. Apparently, I just couldn't stop saying the wrong thing as of late.

"Grayson..." she moaned as I slammed down the cocktail shaker, getting up and putting some distance between us.

"I think I've overstayed my welcome," I

said, sliding my hand in my pocket.

"Grayson, don't—"

"I'll be fine, Giselle. Don't worry about me," I said, needing to get as far away from her and my pain in the ass family as I could.

It wasn't like I lived *that* far away. I was practically right up the road.

In the solitude of my Porsche, I was finally able to breathe, to let out a frustrated breath before turning on the engine.

CHAPTER FOURTEEN

Grayson

I'D HAD EVERY intention of driving home, but somehow, some way, I ended up in the parking lot of M's Place. And I just sat there, staring at the faint glow of the sign against the dusk, watching the doors like somehow they would have the answer. Which clearly didn't make any sense.

Maybe my sister was right. Maybe I wasn't fit to drive. Maybe I should just relax my seat and take a nap until this fucking existential crisis disappeared.

I'd just about settled on reclining when I heard a knock on my window. I jumped up, noticing Henry on the other side.

Was I hallucinating?

I hurriedly rolled the window down. Against the oncoming night, he looked warm and inviting, chocolate brown eyes and shaggy hair blowing in the wind across his tan face.

His perfect, kissable lips parted just the slightest to tease my already sensitive psyche into oblivion.

Fuck, he was *pretty*.

But the warmth radiating from his gaze, from his fucking aura, settled something inside me I couldn't quite put my finger on.

"Hey," he said softly as I gaped at him like a lunatic.

This is becoming a habit.

"Hey," I said, not sure what else to say. I felt on the brink of something, like at any moment my cracks would split and I'd never be able to piece myself back together.

And Henry must have sensed it too, because his eyebrows furrowed as he leaned into my window just the slightest.

"Someone said there was a guy in a Porsche just sitting here, like casing the joint. They wanted to call the police, but..."

Henry swallowed, his gaze flashing to my lips.

"I kinda had a feeling it might be you, and told Max as much."

My gaze drifted to his lips, his jaw. The curve of his arm as he leaned against my driver side door.

"You covered for me?" I asked, my voice breathy, desperate.

I hated it.

Henry cracked a smile. "Yeah, I, uh... guess I did."

"Oh," I said, like an idiot. Completely dumbfounded by his presence.

"Bad night?" he asked softly.

I leaned back against my seat. "You don't know the half of it."

I watched Henry's lips twist, listened as he tapped his fingers on the outside of my car door.

"I, uh... can give you a ride home. You look like you need it."

I sighed, rolling my eyes as I looked up at the ceiling. I didn't really need it. Two drinks wasn't enough to put me under, but I couldn't deny Henry's offer made me want to say yes, if only because I selfishly wanted him in my proximity. I liked being around him, talking to him.

What was happening to me?

I wasn't usually this... this... messy.

"You're working, I—"

"Give me five minutes," he said firmly, pointing at me with his finger like a teacher scolds a child. "Don't move."

I held my hands up in mock defeat. Something about the tone of his voice, the firmness of it, made my blood rush and my damn dick twitch.

Not now, buddy!

"Yes, sir," I drawled as I watched Henry walk away, his dark jeans accentuating the delicious curve of his perfect ass.

A man could get used to a sight like that.

Focus, Gray!

I'd only just shut my eyes, when I heard his voice again.

"Get up, sunshine," he said as he opened the door for me.

For a moment, I stared at him, against the sunset, lit up like some angel.

I'd never been one who liked to be bossed around or told what to do. Too stubborn, too overly confident, too bold. But something inside of me flipped a switch as I listened to Henry without so much as a protest.

Maybe I really am spiraling into chaos.

Hello pre mid life crisis...

I slid into my passenger door, letting Henry in the driver's seat once more.

"I'm taking you home this time," he said as he turned to look at me with an appraising gaze.

I sighed as I brought up the maps feature on my car, watching his gaze fall as he realized home was as easy as a few clicks.

"You could have told me that yesterday," he mused as he pulled out of the parking lot.

"Yesterday, I was a bit... under the weather."

"Mhmm. And what are you today, because you're certainly not above it," he bit out.

"I'm... in the middle of a rather unsettling storm," I said sarcastically.

"Something wrong? You wanna talk about it?" he asked, his voice shaky for some reason.

I turned toward him, taking in the sight of him in my driver's seat, his long, toned arms, the way he grabbed my steering wheel. The way his hair shimmered with streaks of gold as the dying sunlight poured in through the windows.

"A lot of things. But it doesn't matter," I murmured, feeling far too vulnerable and guilty for my own good.

The closer we got to the wedding, the more I seemed to be unraveling.

It seemed like no time at all when we'd finally come to my humble abode. The driveway was still empty, which meant my parents were likely still at my sister's.

Whatever the case, I was glad for the moment at least to have the house to myself, if only to wallow in my sorrows and guilt. Alone.

Before I could open my door, it swung open of its own accord, and I looked up at Henry once more as he offered me his hand.

I wanted to take it.

I wanted to set my palm in his, feel that heat that seemed to brew between us when we touched. But I was also agitated and annoyed, and instead, I pushed it away, opting to get myself out of my car.

I wasn't some damsel in distress, or a passenger prince, thank you very much.

Henry stepped back, giving me a wide

berth to stroll up the driveway toward the door. I didn't expect him to follow me.

But I didn't dislike it either.

We stood on the steps of my porch for a moment, my keys in my hand.

"Do you... want to come in? For a drink?" I asked plainly. I was aware that we were rather close, though I couldn't remember how that happened. Henry stood so close, it would have been easy to reach out and wrap my arms around his trim waist, would have been no trouble at all to slide my fingers through his hair and kiss him like my heart and my opinionated dick wanted to.

But the memory of the previous night reared its head yet again, making me remember just how I'd fucked myself with such behaviors before. I didn't want Henry to think of me as some asshole who got drunk and went around making out with hot guys.

I mean, sure, I'd had my fair share of that, but Henry wasn't just some guy. I wasn't sure what he was really at the time. I could barely process my own feelings, let alone the sparks forming between Henry and I.

"I shouldn't, really, I—"

"Not a drink, drink. I mean, like a... hot tea or something?"

Good God, what was wrong with me?

Had the martinis gone to my brain?

"I mean, I probably should get going. You're okay and..."

"Henry..."

"I should go," he said as he turned away, and I watched him once more like a tall glass of water, held just out of my reach.

And only then did I realize how thirsty I was.

CHAPTER FIFTEEN

Henry

"OKAY, SO THE only thing we're missing really is snacks," Mia said as she ticked off more items on her list.

While I traveled much lighter than my sister, there was a part of me that still felt like an outsider. For starters, some of the wedding party were bringing their significant others—Lane and Lacey obviously came as a pair—not to mention my sister and her boyfriend, and of course, Giselle and Aaron. Even Julie was bringing her beau of only three months, Marcus. Riley, Aaron's brother was even bringing his co-worker!

Not only would I be spending the

weekend—which I couldn't get out of now, because Grayson had taken it upon himself to tell my sister and Giselle that I was indeed coming—with my sister and her well-to-do friends slash party members doing yuppie stuff I had no experience with, but I was going to have to see Grayson all weekend.

Which should have been a good thing, considering the man was like Grade A Certified Eye Candy, but it seemed like every time I got near him, I lost my damn brain.

I couldn't stop thinking about the other night. The night he showed up to M's Place, looking lost. When I drove him home—for real, this time—and how close I was to kissing him on his front porch.

Or when he'd smirked at me at the cafe prior to that, teasing me for being *simple.*

Or when he'd tried to kiss me when he was drunk, or the fact I seemed to have no filter around the man.

"I'm sure there will be enough food to feed an army at this thing," I said as I zipped my suitcase. I probably could have gotten away with just a duffel, but I liked to be prepared, especially if we were going to be staying outdoors in tents. The mountains were usually pretty cold at night.

I'd been camping a few times as a kid, mostly summer camp.

While I wasn't the biggest fan of the woods and hiking, Mia and Giselle said this was *glamping* and not actually camping, but I still didn't want to take any chances.

At least, if all else failed, I knew how to pitch a tent and start a fire. Besides, it was just a weekend. Surely, I could survive a few days in the mountains with my sister and her friends. I'd survived worse.

"Oh, I'm sure there will be, but sometimes it's just nice to have your favorite comfort snacks after a long day of drinking or hiking, you know?" Mia said as she nudged me.

"So just how many bags of hot fries are you bringing then?" I teased.

Mia rolled her eyes. "Obviously the family size bag will be enough to keep me satisfied all weekend," she said, and she stuck her tongue out. "I can't believe we leave tomorrow morning," she said, her lips turning up into a genuine smile.

It was my turn to roll my eyes. "Yup, thrilled."

"It's going to be amazing, Henry, I promise. You're going to have so much fun!" she squealed. "Maybe you'll even meet your own prince charming!"

I sighed as I rolled the suitcase to the side of my couch. "I doubt it, but I'm glad one of us is optimistic," I grumbled.

"You don't give yourself enough credit, you know that, right?" she said as she took a seat next to me, her perfectly highlighted hair bouncing as she did so.

I sighed, knowing the conversation that would follow, and I knew I didn't want to talk about my perpetual singleness.

"Not everyone is your ex," she said softly, and my shoulders fell.

I knew my sister wasn't trying to pry or be a pain in the ass. She genuinely wanted me to be happy, and was my biggest cheerleader in life.

I wanted those things too, but...

"I'm a thirty-one year old man waiting tables at a dive bar, renting an apartment, and I don't even have a fucking goldfish, Mia. Pretty sure I'm a low man on the totem pole."

Mia frowned, her gaze sympathetic. "You never know, maybe you'll meet a Richard Gere type and sweep him off his feet," she teased.

"Please. You'd look much better in a Vivian dress than I do," I shoved her with a laugh, trying to ease my way out of the conversation with compliments. But my sister saw right through me.

"That may be true, but you are a thirty-one year old man who has a heart of gold, who makes enough in tips to afford your rent and then some, and goldfish are a pain in the ass. You have to, like, clean their tank every forty-eight hours or something or they stink to high hell," she said with a grin, and I couldn't help but laugh.

"All I'm saying, is you are way too hard on yourself. Let up a little. Maybe go into this weekend with no expectations, and just... see what happens. For once, don't try to predict the outcome. Live in the moment, Henry."

Her words sunk in, melting my cold heart and resolve just a fraction.

Maybe she was right, maybe I was too hard on myself.

Maybe I did need to just... let go a little

bit.
	Three days.
	I could relax for three days, right?

CHAPTER SIXTEEN

Henry

"FUCK!" I YELLED as panic laced through me. I banged my head against the steering wheel as the dying sounds of my engine echoed in the air.

Of all days for my car to kick the bucket, the morning I was supposed to leave for the damn trip was the day my car decided to say, "Eff you, Henry, we're through!"

It would be just my luck.

I sighed as I called my sister, my stomach twisting, already knowing she would be disappointed, but also, that she probably would just think I'm trying to get out of the weekend altogether.

"Hey Henry, what's up?" she answered, and I could hear voices in the background. She wasn't alone.

"I'm not going to be able to make it," I sighed, waiting for the scolding.

"What? Why? I thought—"

"My car won't start. Like, it won't kick over. At all... I'm going to have to call Triple AAA or something, regardless, but it doesn't look like I'm leaving my driveway. Unless, you're able to pick me up—"

"I can't. I dropped my car off for a recall yesterday and I'm riding with Giselle and Aaron. I'm sorry." She sighed in disappointment, and I felt like the worst fuck up on the planet.

"Does he need a ride?" Giselle's voice shimmered in the background.

"Yeah, his car won't start," Mia said.

"Grayson's driving up by himself. I'll call him, see if he can pick him up."

My blood chilled.

No, it fucking *froze*.

Here lies Henry, frozen like a popsicle.

"That's really not necessary, Mia, I—"

The incoming buzz of a text ominously pulled my attention as Mia asked, "What did you say?"

I swiped up to see Grayson had texted me, "Pick you up in twenty minutes."

I swallowed harshly as I answered Mia.

"Grayson just texted me." The words felt like both a balm and a curse.

"Oh great! I'm so glad that worked out! See you soon, brother!" she said with excitement before hanging up the phone.

I watched with bated breath as the silver Porsche crawled into my parking lot, as the tinted window to the driver's side slid down with ease to reveal Grayson's gorgeous face, his hair swept back with only a few strands falling free in front of his sunglasses.

"Someone call an Uber?" he said with a smirk. His gold watch glinted in the sunlight as he gripped his steering wheel.

Fuck, he was so hot.

Perhaps I was right. Perhaps this was a bad idea all around. Perhaps I could pretend to fall ill. Maybe event faint.

I sure felt like I could as I stared at him in all his GQ-esque glory.

"I don't remember requesting the X model," I said as I dragged my suitcase up the hill. Grayson met me halfway, taking my suitcase from me in a gesture that surprised me. His warm hands against my cold, steady grip was a welcome contrast.

"Well then, today must be your lucky day," he said as he tossed my suitcase in the back of his pristine trunk.

Seriously, whose trunk is that clean?

It's suspicious.

I watched as he slammed it shut, the corners of his lips pulling up into a smirk, before sighing in defeat as I sulked toward the passenger side door.

I attempted to open it, but it wouldn't budge.

With an exasperated sigh, I turned to see Grayson approaching me lazily, reaching his hand out to brush mine away, the feel of his fingertips against the back of my hand sending a chill racing up my spine.

Beep beep.

The mechanical whirring of the locks unlocking sounded and Grayson opened the door with the lightest tug.

"After you, Henry," he said, his voice dark and inviting.

"Thanks," I said, as I crawled in, letting Grayson carefully shut the door and assume his rightful spot in the driver's seat.

CHAPTER SEVENTEEN

Henry

THE ENTIRE WAY to the Brideshead Mountain Resort was complete and utter torment.

For starters, I couldn't stop staring at Grayson the entire ride up—not that there was much else to look at—and I'd already heard Mumford & Sons at least twice in the trip via the satellite radio station, and in my opinion, once was enough.

And clearly, even though I was more than capable of holding a conversation with a hot, annoying asshole, I had apparently lost my last marble, because I found it hard to talk about *anything* but the elephant in the room.

Or more like the elephant trunk in my pants.

I was no stranger to instant attraction, but never in all my years had I been this worked up over just being within close proximity to a man like I was with Grayson.

Not even when I was with my ex... which should have been a clear indicator to me that Grayson was *not* like anyone else.

On the planet.

It was like one touch, one look, was all I needed and *BAM!*

Instant boner.

Which only led me to feel even more insecure and on the spot.

Kill me now.

I glanced at the display as I shifted in my seat yet again, trying to get comfortable and not draw attention to my damn cock.

Think unsexy thoughts...

A feat that was damn near impossible when I was sitting next to the hottest man alive.

The maps on the dashboard showed we were still about an hour away from our destination, and I couldn't help but groan.

It was going to be a long freaking weekend.

CHAPTER EIGHTEEN

Grayson

AFTER THE VALET had taken my car, Henry and I waited for the shuttle alongside the rest of the party, awkwardly.

I'd tried my best to make the ride pleasurable, putting on relaxing music, stirring up conversation, but I'd be lying if I said it was meaningless chatter. Honestly, I was intrigued by Henry and his attitude. Despite our sisters being friends for years, he was truly a mystery to me, but every time I asked a question, Henry either didn't answer, or he answered me with short, curt responses that felt somewhat... personal.

Perhaps he's just in a mood over his car.

After all, an engine that wouldn't start could be a sign it might be time to get a new car. Though I wasn't the best mechanic in the world, I knew that sometimes things were salvageable even when it seemed like they weren't, so I decided to send a message to my car-enthusiast uncle as soon as we touched down. Perhaps he could fix Henry's automobile woes, which would help.

But I won't say anything until I've got confirmation from uncle Bob in the first place. This weekend is supposed to be fun, after all.

While I'd stayed at the Brideshead Mountain Resort before, I hadn't stayed in one of their *glamping* domes, which were still relatively new to the resort. The shuttle to the *glampgrounds* was more or less a small van, decked out inside with modern furnishings. Sleek, oak tables with cup holders and a shared cooler stocked with everything imaginable, it was part RV part party bus, and I was only marginally concerned our glamping domes would be just as tacky. Riley, Aaron's preppy teacher brother and his fellow teacher assistant, Cadence, who he'd brought as his plus one, were jabbering on about his latest trip to Italy with his students, Lane and Lacey were enthralled by the existence of one another again, making moon-eyes at one another, while Julie and her date were involved in some deep conversation with Mia and my sister. For a spacious shuttle, we were all somewhat crammed.

Henry squeezed his suitcase between his legs, crossing his arms.

When we'd finally arrived at the "check-in", it was nothing more than a rustic cabin with a wooden post out front that read *check in.* The post itself was covered in flowers and vines, and the air was a tad bit on the chilly side, but it was only after ten in the morning.

We all piled off the shuttle, dragging our luggage in various states of excitement and involvement. I followed up close to my sister, if only because I wanted to get into my dome and just relax. Have a bit of calm before the storm of planned activities that would undoubtedly transpire. Lord knew my sister probably booked a hiking excursion without giving us all ample time to rest and recharge.

Not all of us functioned with the same amount of energy she did.

When I got to the post, behind her, her shoulders tensed.

"What do you mean you don't have the room? I called ahead of time, with the total headcount... you're *supposed* to have room for twelve people!

"It wasn't mentioned anywhere in our reservation that you wanted two single domes. The reservation says..."

"What's the problem?" Aaron asked as the others filtered in behind us.

I could feel Henry like a ghost behind me, his presence like a magnet, drawing me to turn around and take in his beautiful face, but I had to remain vigilant.

I was not so easily swayed by an emotionally unavailable, bratty, beautiful man.

Was I?

"They don't have the two singles I reserved for Grayson and Henry."

I felt the tension rise like a mercury thermometer behind me at her words, and I couldn't help but sigh.

It seemed I'd fallen into a bout of bad

luck lately where Henry was concerned.

At least, at the time it felt like bad luck, but now...

Now, in hindsight, I could see it was the exact opposite of bad luck.

It was fate.

"You said you have six doubles reserved, correct?" Aaron asked. The concierge nodded, smiling, but I could see the terror behind their eyes. I knew that look well, as my co-workers often wore it when a Bride came in to try her dress on, and the wrong dress had been delivered... because *someone* had typed the wrong thing into the system when it was ordered.

And as a fellow sales guru, I knew just how to placate the poor woman currently worrying she'd be pulled into the manager's office over this.

"Y... yes, but I'm afraid I don't have any single domes available this weekend because of the—"

"Wine Fest," Giselle sighed.

"Henry can stay with me," I said, causing everyone to turn and look at me like I'd grown three heads.

"I mean, it's the logical solution. They already have six domes, and everyone's got a roommate, so..." I shifted my stance, feeling the heat of Henry's gaze. "Just add another mattress or whatever. I'm sure you can do that, right?"

The concierge's shoulders sunk as she shook her head.

"Unfortunately, I can't. As I said, all the doubles and queens were booked out a month ago, and your Rustic Romance Party Package included only suite domes, which all come equipped with one king."

At her words, I caught Henry's gaze, the shock in his eyes as evident as his tense jaw and flushed cheeks.

"Is... is there any vacancy back at the hotel? A cancellation maybe?" he squeaked.

"I'm afraid not, sir," the concierge gently said, and Henry sighed.

"I promise not to steal the covers if you promise not to snore," I taunted him. Henry only had the audacity to look away from me, but I didn't miss the stain of crimson in his cheeks.

I really was a glutton for punishment.

"Well, I guess that settles that then..." Giselle said, looking back at me for a moment.

"Big brother always has a solution,

doesn't he?" Aaron said with a wink.

I rolled my eyes as everyone let out faint laughs.

"Uh huh. One less crisis we have to deal with this weekend," I said, nodding at Henry, adjusting my sunglasses. "Now, can we please get our keys or whatever and get to these God forsaken domes? I'm tired and I'm fucking starving."

CHAPTER NINETEEN

Grayson

THESE FOLKS WEREN'T kidding when they said *dome*. The gigantic, hexagonal glass dome looked like some cross between a spaceship, a greenhouse, and an AirBnB.

And it was entirely exposed, in the middle of the woods. You could see *everything*.

The attendant who shuttled us to our domes walked us up to the front entrance, and tapped the keycard reader before handing us both our individual keycards. "Now as long as you have this on you, as soon as you come in contact with the door, it will unlock."

"It's so..."

"Open..." Henry said nervously.

"Oh, the glass is solar powered. Once the sun starts to go down, the windows turn to shade, which is why we have these—" The man motioned to two lanterns out front on either side of the dome, which were not lit. "Wouldn't want our guests getting lost in the woods in the middle of the night." He chuckled.

"Right," Henry said with a sigh.

"Each dome has its own hotspots with ample WiFi, and is equipped with all the amenities of home. There's four outlets, two on either side of the bed, plus two extra outlets in the kitchen, which includes an espresso machine and a microwave."

"This is not camping," Henry uttered as he stepped inside, looking up at the glass ceiling in awe.

"That's right, sir. This is *glamping*."

"You got that right," I said as I strolled in, setting my suitcase down on the left side of the bed. I watched as Henry slowly walked around, touching the sleek surface of the dressers and countertops like they were made of gold.

"I'll give you time to get settled. The itineraries will be delivered each morning of your stay with the lists of pre-booked activities. Meal times will be in the courtyard, which is about a ten minute walk from your dome. Since you are a party, this section of the woods is reserved and private to just you and your party. Should you wish to make your way back to the hotel, you can call for transport, or it is about a twenty minute hike downhill to the resort itself."

I nodded as the attendant backed away, leaving through the door.

"If you need anything, and I do mean *anything*," he said, his gaze flashing to Henry with warmth, "My name is Cam, and I'm only a phone call away," he said, pointing to the in-dome telephone on my nightstand.

"Thank you, Cam, that'll be all," I said dryly as I dismissed him.

When the door closed, I turned to see Henry already unpacking, his suitcase sprawled across the sleek, shiny wooden floor.

"Henry," I said as I approached him cautiously.

He looked up, his face devoid of any

emotion. "Yeah?" he grunted.

"I know we haven't..." I started, feeling at a loss for how to express what I wanted to say.

It seemed the moment I came near Henry, I lost all my faculties.

But I needed to try, if only because I didn't want the weekend to be awkward.

Or the wedding.

A truce needed to be called.

"I think... we may have gotten off on the wrong foot," I said.

Henry sighed as he set his clothes out neatly on the bed in careful, organized piles.

"Grayson... we don't... we don't have to do this."

"Yes, we do," I said firmly. "I know I haven't given you the best impression of myself. I'm just... this wedding has me coming undone at the seams," I said as I set to unpacking my things on the opposite side of the bed.

We both worked in tandem.

"Aren't weddings supposed to bring people *joy*?" he asked sarcastically.

I smirked. "Apparently for some, it breeds stress."

"And you are part of the one percent

that gets stressed out by weddings?" he asked, turning to arrange his clothes in the dresser. I watched as he did so, noting the slender curve of his arm, the way his shirt rose just enough to show a sliver of skin.

My cock sprang to attention, and I groaned in defeat.

Maybe this was a bad idea.

But what other choice did we have?

The last thing I wanted was for my sister to start out her weekend on a sour note and be miserable the entire time.

"I sell wedding dresses for a living, if anyone knows the stress of weddings, it is me."

"That's an interesting career choice. I would have pegged you for a stock broker or an accountant, or something."

It was my turn to stock the dresser as Henry waltzed over to the kitchen.

"How judgmental of you," I taunted.

Henry turned to appraise me with his gorgeous brown eyes, looking me up and down like I truly was some prize pony, and my cock twitched at the sight.

Never in my life had I wanted someone to *like* me, not the way I wanted Henry to like me. His gaze, his approval, his *praise* was like a drug I didn't know I needed.

"Me? Judge you?"

"You did call me a yuppie," I said, brushing some stray strands of hair out of my eyes as I finished up with the dresser.

"I didn't..." Henry sighed, and we both stood there, a mere distance apart, staring at one another like it was some sort of standoff.

"I'm just... not good at... this." Henry huffed, taking a seat in one of the rustic, cream-colored chairs adorned with a shellacked wooden frame. He set his face in his hands as he let out an exasperated sigh of his own.

"Good at what, Henry?" I asked, truly piqued.

"I've never been good at... fitting in with people. Mia... she's always been a chameleon. She can adapt to wherever she is, whoever she is with. And this life... this... traveling and brunch and lake houses and spa retreats... she's a classic. She fits in. But I don't, I—" He sunk into his chair, and I watched his shoulders fall.

"I don't have anything in common with anyone here. With you," he said sadly. "I'm so out of my element."

Oh, that's what this is about.

I pulled up a chair opposite him, crossing my legs. "Henry, look at me, I want to tell you something," I commanded, and to my surprise, he did just as I asked, without refusal.

So he can be a good boy when he wants to be.

Noted.

"What?" he asked, his lips parted just the slightest. Between his perfect pout, his innocent chocolate eyes, and the look on his face, I knew I was a goner.

Because I'd never felt so *compelled* to let my secrets out, the way I did when I was with Henry.

"I don't fit in either," I whispered.

Henry shook his head. "You're just saying that. You—"

"I'm the literal black sheep in my family, Henry. They *expected* me to be the one to run off into the sunset and have three point five children with a house in the Hamptons and an admirable stock portfolio. But what they got was a son who prefers cock, with a praise kink, who's done nothing but consistently disappoint them, who works a high stress job just so I don't have to be home and be hounded by my parents about what a damn failure I am.”

Henry’s eyebrows furrowed and he rubbed his knees. “Grayson, I—”

“It’s fine. I’m *fine* with my choices in life. I’ve accepted that those things aren’t for me,” I said, feeling strangely vulnerable with the onslaught of baggage I’d just unloaded on Henry.

It was like I had word vomit or something.

Except, I *did* want some of those things.

I wanted Prince Charming to come in and sweep me off my feet, but I’d accepted that probably wasn’t going to happen.

“All I’m saying is, maybe we both shouldn’t judge a book by its cover.”

Henry nodded, pursing his lips. “Right. Fresh start.”

“Fresh start,” I said, just as a knock on the door pulled my attention away.

I rose from my seat, careful to hide my sudden erection as I walked to the door.

Cam stood there, with a cream piece of paper. He handed it to me like it was made of lava.

“What’s this?” I asked dryly.

“This is your itinerary for the *evening*,”

he said with a grin.

I grabbed the paper, letting my gaze rove over the fancily printed sheet.

Lunch in the courtyard in thirty minutes.

Spa Soak and Reflexology at 1:30.
Walk at three pm.
Dinner in the courtyard, served tableside.
Smores & Campfire following.

I let out a sigh of my own as I dismissed Cam once more.

"Thank you, Cam," I said, all but shutting the door in his annoying face.

"What was that all about?" Henry asked.

I turned to see him removing his shirt, headed for the shower. I swallowed harshly at the sight of him, his exposed, tanned, trim chest.

I'd been with plenty of muscle in my day, but there was something about Henry's understated tone, the softness of his hips jutting out from his jeans, that made my already sensitive cock ache with desire.

I shifted my weight, my attention pulled to the beginning of moisture already starting to pebble at my head.

Fuck me sideways.

"Just, uh, our itinerary for the evening. Lunch in the courtyard in thirty minutes," I said.

Henry nodded as he disappeared through the door to the shower, which wasn't large by any means, but it was frosted glass, and therefore, at least it gave enough privacy that I wouldn't have to suffer the sight of a blurred out, naked Henry taunting me and my stiff, leaking cock.

I turned away, grabbing my cock through my chinos as I cursed. Knowing Henry was only a mere feet away, naked was not helping matters.

The sound of water hitting the tile was like a lullaby, and I briefly looked over my shoulder. I couldn't see him from where I had migrated to, on the edge of the king-sized bed, which meant he couldn't see me either.

But I still felt a sense of shame and guilt as I unbuckled my belt, unbuttoning my pants. Considering anyone traipsing around outside would have quite the voyeuristic show if they decided to look in. Thankfully, a quick scan of the windowed perimeter was enough confirmation that

Cam was indeed gone, and no one else was in sight. Still, the idea of someone—particularly a hot, naked someone I was a mere distance from—catching me with my swollen cock in hand, thrilled me more than I care to admit.

For God's sake, if I didn't take care of my unruly cock, I wouldn't be able to think straight. Especially when Henry came out of his afternoon shower.

All wet, tanned, and...

I let my body fall back onto the bed with ease, pulling my cock free. I glanced once more to make sure Henry couldn't see me, and I couldn't see him. I could see the edges of the shower in my vision, the rest of it hidden by potted plants and a rather modern looking partition.

Checkmate.

My feet planted firmly on the ground, my chinos around my ankles, I slipped my hand around my sensitive shaft, using my fingers and thumb to spread the warm, sticky precum over my head, thrusting my hips up against my palm as I began to stroke myself. Despite the fact I couldn't see him from this angle, my mind filled with images of Henry and his soft hips, his tanned chest.

His pouty, perfect lips.

I let my imagination wander, drawing the lines of fantasy once more. It didn't take much, as the thought of Henry in the shower, with his own hand wrapped around his cock, was all I needed to cum, hard and fast.

I slid my hand over my head, if only to minimize my mess and hide the evidence of the shameful self-love session I'd just engaged in with the object of my desire mere feet away. The desire to groan in ecstatic release was prevalent, but I didn't want to draw attention to my guilty masturbation session.

I struggled to catch my breath, to keep my moans stifled down deep inside, as I stuffed my softening, wet cock back in my boxers, hurriedly heading toward the kitchen—complete with a sink—and washed away my sins, just as the tinkling waterfall sounds diminished, and the sound of the shower door opened.

That was fucking close.

I nonchalantly zipped and buttoned my pants before turning to see Henry, towel around his waist, water gleaming on his bronzed skin, dark, wet hair falling in his beautiful eyes, and I was more than thankful I came already.

Because I was certain if I hadn't, I would have right there.

Henry truly was a sight for sore eyes.

"Are you... showering before lunch or—" His cheeks pinkened as his gaze roved over me.

I shook my head. "Well, seeing as how we are down to fifteen minutes, I say probably not. Cam said the courtyard is about a ten minute walk, so we should probably leave as soon as possible."

Henry nodded. "Yeah, of course. I'll be ready in a sex... I mean *sec*!"

He spun around, but I didn't miss the scarlet flushing his cheeks as I let out a laugh.

How he didn't know he was so very right indeed.

CHAPTER TWENTY

Grayson

I LET THE water run over me, my hands braced against the stone wall. The heat and steam felt good, especially after sitting for the last few hours outdoors.

Not to mention, I was still overly stuffed from dinner.

Though after spending the evening mostly sneaking glances at Henry—who'd been avoiding me all night by talking to his sister and her beau—I was more than frustrated.

But I also had to remember that Henry didn't really owe me anything, and talking to people who actually knew him, well, was probably a sort of comfort.

But damn it if I wasn't jealous.

I wanted to be the center of Henry's attention.

That wasn't like me, at all. I didn't chase after men, nor did I throw myself at their feet.

But I would have thrown myself over the fire pit and roasted my ass like a marshmallow if it would have caught Henry's attention, which is why I'd taken it upon myself to leave the party early. Both me and my unruly cock had had enough taunting for one night.

Besides, it would probably be best to be by myself if only so I could take care of said frustrations and just pass the fuck out.

No doubt my sister had us scheduled for an early rise. Something I was *not* looking forward to.

Honestly, I barely registered anything except the sound of the water, and my own relief. I breathed much easier as I let out a deep groan, watching my release as it slid down the drain, along with my pent up frustrations.

I turned the water off, pulling the towel off the rack and wrapping it around my waist. In the dome, it was quiet, save for the melodies of easy listening jazz coming from my phone. Opening the door, I grabbed my phone, padding out of the bathroom, and almost stopped in my tracks as I laid eyes on Henry.

Who was in nothing but Star Wars printed pajama pants, on top of the bed.

Browsing his phone, but...

Panic laced through me as I wondered how long he'd been there.

What if he'd been there when I...

Or perhaps he'd been too engrossed with his phone.

"When... when did you get here?" I asked plainly as I headed over to my dresser.

Henry's gaze shot up to me immediately, his eyes darkening. "I literally just came," he said, his voice breaking into a cough as he shook his head. "Came in the door, I mean."

"I see," I said, watching his pink tongue dart out to trace over his lips.

A part of me wanted to drop my towel right there and really give him something to lick, because the unexpected heat that had formed in his gaze was driving me wild.

It was almost as if... as if maybe, Henry felt this undeniable connection too.

But I got the feeling Henry wasn't the type to take risks, so I needed to tread carefully.

"Any... anyway, I was just setting my alarm," he said hurriedly, keeping his gaze fixed on mine as I pulled out my boxers from the dresser. I made a point to hold his gaze as I dropped my towel, waiting to see if he'd take the bait.

Henry bit his lip, swallowing harshly, but he didn't look. Not even a glance.

Though by the scarlet flush in his cheeks, he didn't need to.

Well, I'll be damned.

"Can you believe my sister expects us all up at the ass crack of dawn? It's absurd! We are supposed to be relaxing..." I said, snapping the band on my boxers until they smacked my skin.

Henry pulled his legs up, crawling underneath the covers as he looked away. "Yeah... right. Relaxing," he said with a sigh as he lay on his side, presenting his back to me as he touched the base of his lamp on his side, making the room darken.

And just like that, the spell was

broken, and Henry had clammed up once more.

I sighed in defeat. Judging from Henry's reaction, I knew perhaps he felt *something*. I just wasn't sure if it was something he wanted to act on. Though why he would fight such feelings, I did not know, but I garnered whatever the reason was, it must be a good one. No one goes through life with walls like that unless they'd been shattered before.

Which made me want to find the man responsible for such atrocities and give him a piece of my mind.

"Goodnight, Grayson," Henry murmured as I slid into my side of the bed, careful to leave an ample amount of space between us. A part of me wanted to pry, to press. To tell him it was okay, he didn't have to hide from me, but as I opened my mouth, I heard the softest sound coming from him.

Almost like a purr.

I watched the rise and fall of his shoulders as he breathed, his breath slow and steady, and the sound of his soft snores filling the quiet air. The light from my side illuminated him.

I didn't know Henry well yet, but I

knew he deserved every bit of light and happiness this world had to offer, and whoever had made him think otherwise would get their just desserts.

Karma, and all.

Suddenly, exhaustion hit me and the sound of his soft snores were almost melodic, hypnotizing even. I couldn't help but smirk, knowing there was no use fighting the slumber I was about to fall into.

"Goodnight, Henry," I whispered as I touched the lamp on the nightstand.

CHAPTER TWENTY-ONE

Henry

I CURLED CLOSER to the warmth that surrounded me. The air smelled faintly of lavender and sage, a most relaxing scent. I fell into that scent, into the pit of warmth. I hadn't felt so relaxed in a while, and certainly not since Grayson showed up the other night.

Grayson...

His name filled my consciousness, along with thoughts of his perfect lips, of his dark, inviting eyes, and that dead-sexy smirk he was always wearing. I shifted my position closer to the fire, groaning in satisfaction. I could feel the head of his cock brushing against my ass, and I let out a deep groan as I arched my back, seeking more of the friction.

My own cock was already alert and aware, no doubt reeling from my sexy dream state. Warm fingers slid over the waistband on my pajama pants, a leg threading through mine as he pulled me closer.

I didn't want the dream to end, but my alarm broke the veil of ecstasy.

I reached out instinctively to shut it off, and then I realized in absolute horror, I wasn't asleep, and I certainly wasn't dreaming.

My hand hovered over my phone as my gaze settled on a hand across my stomach, and I felt the vivid, sizeable hardness pressed against my ass.

"Oh my God," I said as I scrambled out of Grayson's hold, smacking my alarm much more harshly than I meant to.

"Oh my God, I am so sorry, Grayson. I—"

"Good morning to you too, Henry," he grumbled as I threw myself out of bed.

I quickly tried to readjust myself, embarrassment flooding me. I looked at Grayson, fueling up another apology, but all my speech left me when I noticed

Grayson's gaze roving over me, stopping right where I was holding my—

"I'm not a... morning person," I stammered.

What the fuck?

Grayson laughed, the sound smooth and warm, showcasing his perfect teeth as he sat up, the covers sliding off of him to reveal his perfectly defined chest.

"Could have fooled me," he said, his gaze flicking back up to my reddening cheeks, then back to my hands still awkwardly shielding my noticeable erection from him.

"It's not... I didn't mean to—"

Grayson ran his hand through his dark hair. "Please, don't be embarrassed. We're both adults."

Yeah, single adults.

Who are supposed to be starting fresh!

And not making things awkward!

I was acutely aware that I was once again, making things awkward, but I couldn't help it. It was like my damn superpower or something.

I swallowed harshly as I looked back at him. "I need a shower," I mumbled. Clearly with all the blood rushing to my cock, my brain was not working at full capacity.

"Henry..." He sighed as he let his head fall back against the headboard.

I turned around, making a beeline directly for the shower, if only for the space to breathe, to process what had just happened.

Grayson and I... spooned.

Granted we were probably asleep when we gravitated toward one another, but still...

I'd awakened with Grayson's arms around me and his cock pressed against me, and I didn't hate it.

In fact, I kind of liked it, if I'm being honest, but I didn't have time for romantic revelations at six thirty in the morning.

I turned the water on, relieved by the crisp, cool sensation. I braced myself for the shiver, knowing it was most certainly what I needed to wash away all the embarrassment and the desire swirling inside of me like a hurricane.

I quickly washed my hair with the shampoo provided, which smelled like lemongrass and cedar and was actually quite invigorating. After I'd finally finished up, I grabbed my towel, and headed for the main room, doing my best to avoid staring at shirtless Grayson in his *boxers*, looking like an Esquire magazine spread.

But I was weak, apparently, because the moment I came out to see him, his perfect ass on display, standing there like a Greek Adonis staring at a paper in front of a literal cart of breakfast items, I froze.

Cue Henry Popsicle Mode.

"What—"

"Breakfast is served," Grayson drawled.

"Apparently, my sister had a spread delivered to all our tents this morning," he said as he looked up from his paper.

"Oh, well... that's kinda nice, actually," I said as I turned my back to him, fishing out a pair of underwear, cargo pants, and an olive green shirt.

"No doubt to make up for the fact we are *horseback* riding at eight in the morning," he grumbled.

"Horseback riding?" I asked as I pulled on my shirt. I could feel Grayson's eyes on me, and I fought to turn around and meet his gaze.

"Did I stutter?" he asked, his voice dark and smooth.

I turned around, weak to fight my own

impulse to find him only inches away from me. There I stood in my shirt and my fresh pair of boxer briefs, acutely aware of his disheveled hair, of his looming, sexy stare, and the visible outline of his cock.

How was this man still single?

He was quite literally, all the things fantasies were made of.

What flaw did he have?

Because as far as I could see or discern, there were none.

Grayson was confident, sexy, and more than sure of himself. But he was also candid and vulnerable, and mysterious.

He was everything a prince charming should be.

And he was so close I could touch him. That I could kiss him, if I wanted, and I wanted to, but...

Did *he* want me to?

Despite his flirtations, and his drunk pass at me the other night, he hadn't made a move to confirm such things. In fact, he'd only done the opposite and insisted on a "fresh" start. But then it seemed every time the curtain came down...

I wasn't sure if I'd purely imagined the attraction between us, or if it was something that truly was reciprocated. But I wasn't capable of voicing my wonders out loud when I didn't have a full grasp on the reality myself.

"No, you did not," I said, my own voice dropping an octave, my gaze falling to his lips.

All it would take is one small move. One step forward and I could slide my hand over his hip, or run my fingers through his hair.

One gentle tug and I could pull him toward me, toward my lips.

But I was afraid.

Of what I wasn't certain.

"Shower's all yours," I said, my voice steady as I flashed my gaze from his perfect pout to his intense amber eyes.

Grayson smirked as he handed me the itinerary, and I watched him walk away from me, sliding his boxers off just before he hit the door so I could get just the slightest glimpse of his bare ass.

While the move was careless, as undressing for a shower was a normal action, his move felt deliberate.

It was almost like he *wanted* me to see him, like he wanted to taunt me with his perfection.

EVIE RILEY

Look at what you can't have because you're too fucking scared.

I grunted as I adjusted my cock, turning away from the sight in favor of breakfast.

The sun shone through the hexagonal windows like beams of heaven, lighting up the champagne flutes full of champagne and orange juice, no doubt, across the array of bear claws and croissants and pastries with fresh fruit.

I wasted no time as I dug into the cream cheese danishes and fresh strawberries, watching the light cast rainbow prisms on the inside of our dome as I waited for the bane of my literal existence.

CHAPTER TWENTY-TWO

Henry

IF YOU'VE NEVER been on a horse before, nothing can truly prepare you for the experience. For starters, I was surprised at the sheer size of the horse before me, and the way he looked me in my eye, snorting and huffing, I couldn't deny I was panicking.

"Have you ever ridden a horse before?" Grayson asked as he came up behind me. I watched as Lane helped his partner up on her horse, watched as she threw her leg over the saddle.

Mia and Giselle spent a lot of time together as teens, and I'd heard the stories she'd told about Giselle's horse. I even remembered when she asked our parents for a horse for her birthday, which they clearly denied.

Though she hadn't bought her own horse yet, she regularly visited the barn where Giselle used to board her childhood horse, and once in awhile, I knew she would take a ride.

But I had no such experience, and therefore, I felt out of my element.

"No," I said with a sigh, turning to see Grayson's intense gaze roving over me once more.

"I can just... sit this out. Wait for you guys to come back."

"Absolutely not," Grayson shook his head, just as Mia came over to us, on her *horse.*

"I'm so excited for you!" she beamed.

"Don't be, I was just telling Grayson I think I'm going to sit this out."

"And I told you that is not an option," Grayson said, crossing his arms.

"What did I tell you about *new experiences*, Henry?" Mia said with a scolding glare.

"Yeah, well, some new experiences are clearly not for beginners."

"You do as I say and I promise you you'll be master of the saddle in no time," Grayson said, smirking at me with that delicious pout of his, stirring up all the desire and pent up frustration all over again.

"I don't have a choice, do I?" I sighed.

Grayson shook his head, his smirk widening. "Fast learner," he said as he motioned for me to follow him to the open stables where Julie and her date were getting ready on their horses, leading *my* horse to a spot that looked open enough we could have space for me to embarrass myself fully and probably fall off.

This was a nightmare.

"Okay, so first things first... the horse can smell your fear," he said as he looked at me.

"I'm not afraid—" I lied.

Grayson only had the audacity to raise an eyebrow at me.

"There's nothing to be afraid of. The horse is a gentle creature. He only responds to your insecurity, your fears. You are in control, and he will follow *your* lead. So, trust yourself."

I swallowed harshly as his words fell on me.

"If only it were that easy," I mumbled.

Grayson ran his hand along the horse's hide, until he came to the saddle.

"It is easy," he said as he patted the saddle. "When you have a good teacher," he said warmly. "Besides, once you're up there, on top—"

It was his turn for his cheeks to redden for once, but I wasn't entirely sure it wasn't due to the wind.

"Once you're holding the reins, you'll know what to do."

I watched Grayson adjust my saddle, like a true master. It was both shocking and interesting to see him in his element, doing something he was clearly passionate about. His confidence with the horse was much different than the Grayson I'd seen thus far.

"Now, step here," he said as he motioned for me to place my foot in the stirrup. "Set your hand on me if you need to steady yourself, and swing your leg over the saddle until you've found the stirrup on the other side."

I did as he requested, knowing everyone was waiting on me, and not wanting to hold anyone up. I pursed my lips as I set my foot in the stirrup, bracing one hand on his shoulder, and using the other to hold the handle of the saddle. I hoisted my leg up—rather ungracefully—just as he instructed, fumbling with the stirrup on the other side. But I managed, nonetheless, turning to look at Grayson, who was smirking at me again.

"Very good," Grayson said. "It's good to know you can be broken too." His tone was dark, gravelly, and made my cock stiffen just the slightest. Despite being uncomfortable, I was glad the saddle and my vantage point hid such things.

Before I could bite back at Grayson's sexual innuendos, he cleared his throat and left me to my own devices. Mia and her horse trotted over to me, as I attempted to grab my reins.

Grayson had been right, but I wasn't going to tell him that. Being on top of my horse felt... nice. The vantage point was pretty, but also there was a peacefulness I didn't know I'd experience. My sister tried her best to give me tips, and I tried my best to listen, but I couldn't focus entirely because the sight of Grayson—who was wearing tight, riding pants and a form-fitting long sleeve—was too much to tear my sights from.

I watched the way he mounted his horse, in one fell swoop, knowing he'd probably done this before a million times. But something about watching him felt like it was the first time. And I was captivated by the way he administered his control. How boldly he gripped the reins, his commanding voice.

He trotted up next to his sister, only looking over his shoulder once at my sister and I, his dark eyes commanding me the same way he did his horse.

Let me lead.

My cock and I were powerless to resist, and so I gripped my reins and followed Grayson into the woods like a lamb to the slaughter.

CHAPTER TWENTY-THREE

Henry

THE RIDE THROUGH the mountains was a lot better than I expected. Aside from the sound of the horses neighing and trotting, there was a serenity to the woods. Birds tweeting and chirping and small animals skittering through bushes. Our ride took most of the day, and I came to learn that the trail we were riding led us through seven waterfalls.

To say it was breathtaking would be an understatement, and I started to think perhaps my sister was right. Maybe I did need to just let myself *enjoy* things, rather than over think them. So that was exactly what I had vowed to do the rest of the day, and the rest of the weekend.

Just... enjoy the moment.

The relaxing air as my horse and I trotted through the woods, the beauty of nature. I even enjoyed talking to Aaron and his best man, Riley, a little bit about their travels and the places they'd been. The places I'd *like* to see someday.

Though it seemed as if the tables had flipped, because the more comfortable I became in my current environment, the more comfortable I got with the conversations and the people, Grayson seemed to do the exact opposite. Aside from his flirtatious training earlier, he kept to the front of the group, leading us with Giselle, but he was mostly quiet.

A part of me wondered if it was something I said or did, but Mia had informed me Grayson was usually quite stoic when he rode. I wasn't sure if sisterly DNA told her I was pining on the inside, or if she was genuinely just trying to pry about my feelings toward Grayson. She always did have a knack for pulling the things out of me I refused to tell anyone.

CHAPTER TWENTY-FOUR

Henry

I WATCHED THE fire dance as we all surrounded ourselves around it. After a most delicious dinner of fire-roasted beef and vegetables that probably cost more than my luggage, we were served with an array of after-dinner drinks and fireside desserts. Where s'mores were a staple at all the campfires apparently, there were other desserts to choose from.

I'd always been a simple man, something Grayson taunted me about, of course, but even then, when I expected him to say something, he was rather quiet.

Perhaps he is just having an off day or something.

I sipped my warmed *Glühwein,* a concoction Giselle told me derived from the Germans and was quite popular around the holidays, relishing in the sweetness of the mulled spices and the burn of the heated alcohol as it coated my throat and warmed me from the inside.

It truly was the best drink I'd had, and it was perfect to sip around the campfire in a copper mule mug amidst the chilly mountain air.

Thanks to the WiFi available in the glampgrounds, Julie was able to access her Spotify, and graciously provided us with a playlist that was probably as chaotic and unhinged as she was.

Seriously, I was not a fan of *Axe 2 Grind* or Taylor Swift, but I wasn't the one controlling the tunes.

The sounds of Willow and The Anxiety's *Meet Me At Our Spot* swept through the air, the singers crooning on about being hypnotized by the lights, and I couldn't help but look up from my current marshmallow sandwich, catching sight of Grayson lit up by the strings of outdoor lights, grumbling over his burnt marshmallow, twisting his lips in frustration.

I couldn't take my gaze off of Grayson, who sat more or less by himself, away from the rest of us.

I didn't like seeing Grayson like this.

Removed, quiet.

Alone.

Maybe it was because I knew what it felt like to *be* alone, maybe it was because Grayson had told me that he felt like an outcast too.

Or maybe it had something to do with the three glasses of *Glühwein* I'd had.

I assembled the rest of my perfect s'more and walked over to where he sat. Immediately, his gaze flashed up at me, and I could have sworn he looked surprised. I handed him my s'more.

"You look like you need this more than me," I said.

Grayson hesitated for a moment. "Is this a trick?" he said, narrowing his eyes as his fingers grazed mine, taking the chocolaty marshmallow treat.

"No trick. I just... noticed your marshmallow skills seem a little... beginner," I said, flashing him a smirk. Thanks to the wine, I felt a bit better than

I usually did. I found myself just talking instead of trying to constantly figure out the right thing to say.

Or what not to say.

"Well, we all have our skills, it seems," he said as he bit into the s'more, the marshmallow caving and exploding as he groaned.

Same marshmallow, same.

I picked up his stick before heading over to the dessert cart that boasted all the ingredients for everything from s'mores to hand pies to banana boats. I grabbed some marshmallows, noticing how everyone else was in their own little bubbles with one another. Laughing, singing, dancing. Drinking.

When I came back to the lonely log that Grayson was taking up residence on, I slowly set to fixing his stick—and my own—with their prospective sweets.

"It's all in the wrist," I said, motioning to him as I held the stick, to watch how I turned my wrist and not the stick itself. "You want to make sure you get at least ten seconds on all four sides."

"A marshmallow does not have sides," Grayson grumbled, but his tone was marginally lighter.

GRAYSON

I gazed back at him with a confident smirk of my own. "Everyone has sides," I said, realizing my error far too late.

Grayson's shoulders loosened, and I didn't even bother to correct myself.

How could I, when it seemed it was the right thing to say?

I handed him his stick and he took it from me with ease.

"All in the wrist, huh?" He cocked a smile.

The heat in his tone was like a spark to dry kindling. Normally, I agonized over socializing like this.

Innuendos, flirtations, jokes.

But after a few drinks, and being near Grayson—a man who seemed to unravel me whether I wanted him to or not—I couldn't help but respond.

"As you said, we all have our skills, *Grayson*."

Did I really just say that?

Grayson let out a dark chuckle as he rose, heading for the fire to roast his marshmallow, and I followed. Taking my spot beside him, I didn't realize how close I was until I bumped his shoulder.

"Sorry," I said instinctively.

Grayson shifted his stance as he

leaned closer to the fire, watching his marshmallow intently. "Trying to throw me into the fire now are you?" he teased.

I shifted my stance, bumping into him again, smiling at his tone before reaching out and gently turning his wrist.

The touch itself was warm, and not at all sexual.

I was, after all, just helping him with his sub-par roasting skills.

But something about the way his skin felt beneath my fingertips reminded me of the warmth of his hand over my stomach, of his body curled around mine, and I let out a small gasp. I brushed the underside of his wrist rhythmically with my thumb, and swallowed harshly.

I knew I should let go, but...

I didn't *want* to let go.

Grayson didn't move either. Instead, his gaze fell to where I held his wrist.

I gently turned it again, gazing back at the fire, watching as the white sides of the marshmallow turned golden with just the swiftest of motions.

"Not everything is perfect on the first try," I said softly, pulling back.

Grayson followed my lead.

I dropped my hand, nodding toward

the perfectly golden marshmallow, which sported an even color on all sides.

"Some things take time," I said with a shrug, setting to roast my own marshmallow.

My stomach flipped, but I wasn't sure if it was from the alcohol, or the way Grayson was looking at me.

He assembled his s'more as I finished roasting my marshmallow. Pulling the giant toasted piece of fluff off of the stick, melted marshmallow spread along my fingers. I quickly tossed the sticky, melty confection in my mouth, licking my fingers clean, if only because I hated to feel sticky.

The sounds of Post Malone's *Circles* came on over the speakers, and I noticed the rest of the party had decided dancing was apparently a good idea.

Giselle and Aaron wrapped their arms around one another, lost in each other's eyes, and the rest of the couples followed suit. For a moment, it felt like I was witnessing something private, and the reality of my singleness spread once more.

I hadn't danced with anyone in years.

Five years, to be exact.

My gaze drifted to Grayson, who was

staring into the fire like it held all the answers to the questions he didn't dare ask out loud.

I mean, it was a dance, right?

It didn't mean anything. When in Rome and all that...

"We should join them," I said without thinking.

Grayson turned to me, his gaze studying me. "What did you say?"

"I said, we should join them. I mean, it's just dancing, right? Fun shouldn't be something that is only reserved for couples." I shrugged.

I looked back at him in question. "I mean, unless marshmallows aren't the only area you're lacking in skill."

Why did I just insult him?

What the fuck is wrong with me?

I knew the answer to my thoughts as my head was currently spinning.

"That depends," Grayson smirked as he set his hand on my waist, pulling me closer into his hot, sexy vortex.

I slid my hands up his chest, resting them on his shoulders.

"On what exactly?" I asked, my voice unfamiliar, even to me, filled with a darkness I didn't know I was capable of.

GRAYSON

Grayson's hand slid over my hip, resting at my back as he *gently* pressed his palm against me, coaxing me closer.

Pressed against him I could feel *everything.*

My breath caught in my throat as my own cock sprang to attention against the sizeable outline of his hardness.

"If you'll let me lead," he said darkly.

"Maybe that's what I need," I murmured, feeling lightheaded as he swayed us back and forth. I leaned against him, staring up at his dark eyes with wonder, drunk and under his spell.

I hadn't been this close to anyone in a long time, and the reality was slightly terrifying.

I could feel myself falling for Grayson and that scared me.

How was it possible to fall for a man I barely knew in only a matter of days?

My hand slid over his chest, over his heart, and somehow that made it real.

Grayson leaned his face down just the slightest, his gaze full of heat and confidence.

And suddenly, I was faced with the reality that I hadn't *been* with anyone in years, and my insecurities got the best of me. My heart racing, my throat tight, my cock aching for release, and sweat forming all along my body where he touched me, mixed with the fact that we weren't truly alone—and everyone could see us. I panicked.

I pushed away from Grayson, breaking our hold. "I can't do this, I—"

"Henry..."

"I'm sorry," I said, flustered as I did the only thing I could think of.

I ran.

What I didn't expect, was for Grayson to follow me.

Away from the courtyard, the woods were dark. The faint glow from the string lights cast just enough light I could see the tree I almost ran into. I stopped, dropping my hands to my knees as I tried to catch my breath.

"Henry!" Grayson called, and I stood, slowly turning to see the disappointment on his face I knew would be there.

Why did I keep fucking everything up?

Perhaps I was cursed.

Cursed to be a perpetual cockblock to myself for all eternity.

"You are infuriating, do you know that?" Grayson growled.

My eyes widened. "Me?" I snapped back.

He ran a hand through his hair, his gaze dark under the shadows, his lips pressed into a thin line.

"Yes, you! You push me and pull me, only to push me away when I get too close. I'm tired of playing these games with you, Henry. Tired of wondering if you feel this too. Tell me you don't and I'll leave you alone and never ask again."

"This is not on me!" I hollered back. "You and your constant flirtations are maddening, do you know that!"

"Me? You're going to pin this on *me*? Are you insane?" he barked.

"Yeah, I am! Because you tease and taunt me, with your fucking pretty face and your killer body, and... your touch, and... but you don't have the fucking balls to actually follow through, and do something about it—"

Grayson grabbed my face between his hands, crushing his lips to mine in a brutal flurry.

Every bone in my body stiffened as it took a moment for me to comprehend what had just happened. Almost instantly, I melted in his grip as some switch inside me flipped.

I slid my hands into his hair, gripping his silky locks as I parted my mouth, my tongue stroking his in a desperate attempt to find my footing, my grounding. Grayson's grip on my face was fierce, and I ground my hips against him, my cock desperate for the friction of his hardness.

Grayson groaned in my mouth as he thrust himself against me, eliciting a deep, satisfied sound to escape my throat.

And then he broke away, his labored breath the only sound I could hear.

"Am I being fucking clear now, Henry?" he growled, his grip on my face easing up slightly as he tried to catch his breath.

"Crystal, *Grayson,*" I said as I slid my hands out of his hair.

CHAPTER TWENTY-FIVE

Grayson

"GREAT. NOW THAT we've cleared that up, let's head back to the fire," I said, my voice softening, and I could hear the relief in it.

Henry gazed up at me with a mixture of understanding, and hope.

"I— I think I need some air," he said quietly. "I'm just, uh... I think I'm going to head back to the tent."

My heart broke, but a part of me understood. So much had happened between us, and it was apparent that up until moments ago, Henry hadn't understood I truly *wanted* him. And maybe I hadn't understood what that meant either, or the depth of it.

Maybe Henry wasn't the only one who needed space to process everything.

"Okay. Be careful," I said, my voice shaking. All I wanted was to stop him from walking away.

Because unbeknownst to Henry, he held my heart in his hands, and I was trusting he would not shatter it completely.

Henry nodded. "Of course," he said as he slid his phone out, queuing up his flashlight. And I watched him wander off, watched him leave, with my heart in my throat.

Once he was out of my sight, I headed back to the courtyard. It appeared that Henry wasn't the only one who had decided to turn in.

The only ones left at the campfire were my sister, Aaron, and Riley. Riley and Aaron were, of course, engaged in a deep conversation about something I had no clue about, and my sister was sipping her hot chocolate in front of the fire.

I took my seat beside her for the first time since we'd arrived back from our ride.

"So, that's what's had you all out of

sorts lately," she nonchalantly drawled, not even looking at me.

I wanted to deny her allegation, but we both knew there was no denying it. Anyone with eyeballs would have been able to see the flames between Henry and I, especially after his dramatic exit.

Whether or not they would draw attention to it was still unclear, but for Henry's sake, I hoped they wouldn't. I got the feeling that Henry didn't like attention.

"It's complicated," I said, folding my hands in my lap.

Giselle scoffed, shooting me an *are you serious* glance.

"What?" I asked.

"What is this? An episode of *The Young & The Restless*? Relationships aren't complicated."

I sighed, opening my mouth to protest, but my sister stopped me.

"That's just a crock of shit explanation for when things aren't going the way you want them to," she said.

I stared into the fire, watching the ochre flames dance and change shape swiftly.

"Did you ever just... meet someone and

the timing was off? Like... way off?" I asked quietly.

My sister slurped her hot chocolate annoyingly, making me wait for her answer. "Not everything is perfect from the get-go, Gray. Some things..." She looked off in the distance, her gaze settling on her fiancé, who was laughing with his best man, and I didn't miss the glaze of love in her eyes. "Good things take time."

Her words settled on me, making me think about this whole situation. I'd known of Henry for years, but it wasn't until the other night, that I really truly *saw* him. That night, I'd been an idiot and gotten carried away, and Henry had shown me his true colors. He was caring, and sweet, and easy to talk to, and I enjoyed being around him.

And he wasn't bad on the eyes at all.

But the reality was that we'd only really started to discover one another, let alone our undeniable attraction, and it had barely been two weeks.

Falling in love with a man in that short of an amount of time was impossible, wasn't it?

Was what I felt for Henry *love?*

It was, but I wasn't ready to admit that yet. If I was being honest, I fell for Henry the moment I looked at him in my car.

And then I fell for him again when he'd gotten a *simple* sandwich and soup, and again when he stood on my porch, gazing at me like I was some hero in a romance movie.

And there were so many moments after that too, and I got the feeling those moments would never disappear. If we went through with this—whatever *this* was—I was certain there would be so many more moments to fall in love with Henry.

If he would let me.

"Yeah, well, good things also need their beauty rest," I said as I took her empty cup from her hands. Giselle looked at me with annoyance, but I shook my head. "It's getting late, and if I read the itinerary correctly, we have a wine festival tomorrow." I said, flashing her a grin.

"Gray..."

"We're going to need all the rest we can get if we're going to be drinking all day long," I teased.

My sister looked as if she wanted to press me further on matters that had nothing to do with wine, but she relented, admitting defeat for once.

Maybe she really does need a good night's sleep.

"Mhmm. Well, in that case, perhaps you should head to bed too. Some of us need more of a recharge than others," she nipped.

"What's that supposed to mean?" I bit back.

Giselle rose, smiling from ear to ear. "Well, I am the younger model..." she teased.

I shook my head. "The best wines, my dear, are the ones that have *aged* gracefully," I said with a grin of my own.

Giselle laughed. "Sure, whatever makes you sleep better at night," she said as I rose. Giselle wrapped her arms around me, and I could not help but do the same. "Goodnight, Gray," she said softly, as she headed toward Aaron, who was putting out the fire.

CHAPTER TWENTY-SIX

Grayson

I DON'T KNOW why I was so nervous, standing on the precipice of the glamping tent. But my heart was racing as the automatic locks clicked, and I opened the door. Though the sight of shirtless Henry, laying on top of the covers, reading a book—with a handsome, shirtless man on the front nonetheless—settled every nerve in my body.

He did not look up at all, completely engrossed in his tale, and I cautiously approached my dresser. I stood in front of it, and even though I could not see him, I could feel the heat of his gaze.

I removed my shirt first, before tackling my riding pants, which were doing nothing to quell the desire that had already started to percolate at the sight of shirtless Henry in gray sweatpants, reading a book.

Simple things, indeed.

I slid my pants off, turning to catch his deep brown eyes gazing at me over his book.

Shifting my stance, I smirked at him over my shoulder, noticing his gaze was fixated on my ass.

"See something you like?" I teased.

Henry's gaze flashed to mine, blinking only a few times before he tugged his book higher to hide the flush in his cheeks. But I caught just enough scarlet to know his rebuttal of "no," was a damn lie.

And for the moment, that was enough.

My sister had mentioned good things took time, and I knew Henry was a good thing.

Waiting wasn't easy for me, but if it was what Henry needed in order to feel comfortable with *this*, with me...

I'd wait as long as it took.

I took my time folding my clothes and

setting them aside. The world outside us was dark, and the lights of the dome were not bright at all. In fact, the amber glow that touched everything made the dome itself feel far more intimate. It was almost as if we truly weren't in the middle of the woods. It was like our own private bubble.

I pulled down the sheets, sliding in easily as I lay on my side. I slid closer to Henry, if only to try and discern what it was he was actually reading, checking out the book cover.

"What are you doing?" he asked, fidgeting on top of the covers, but he did not squirm away from me as he had this morning.

"What are you reading?" I asked, and Henry's eyes narrowed as he clutched his book to his chest.

"I'll tell you under one condition," he said evenly.

I leaned on my arm, flipping my hair out of my eyes as I gazed up at him. From this angle, he looked positively ravishing. His dark hair was slightly messy, the amber lights casting a golden glow on his eyes and his natural tan skin. The light grey of his sweatpants contrasted with the softened edges of his hips deliciously. My heart raced, all the blood in my body pooling directly in my stiffening cock as the thought of being *underneath* this man ravaged me.

I wanted to see this man come undone, and I wanted to be his inevitable undoing as well.

I wanted to watch him writhe beneath me. I wanted to push him right up against the edge, to drive him as mad as he drove me.

And then I wanted to watch his face as he came, knowing the pleasure was all mine.

Mine.

"Anything," I breathed, far too desperate for my own ears, but I didn't care. I found the more time I spent in Henry's presence, I didn't care how I sounded, or what I looked like, or what I said.

"You have to *promise* you won't judge me," he said, raising his eyebrow.

"Of course, I won't I—"

"Promise!" he said seriously.

I rolled my eyes, showcasing my crossed fingers in surrender. "Scout's honor," I said.

Henry sighed, closing his book, setting

it over his lap as he pulled his legs up to his chest.

"It's about this guy who buys a house and it's haunted," he said, gulping nervously.

"And..."

"And the ghost that haunts it is a really sexy gay ghost from, like, the 1900s."

The urge to laugh was apparent, but I had promised him I wouldn't. I pursed my lips. "That's... interesting." I said, keeping my expression stoic.

"I knew it, you think it's stupid," he said rolling his eyes. "I can see it in your eyes, you want to laugh."

I slid a little closer, and Henry didn't budge. I slowly, deliberately pulled the book from his lap, looking over the cover and the synopsis.

"I don't think anything you do is stupid, Henry," I murmured as I flipped through the pages, stopping on a random page to skim it.

Henry's breathing increased, and I realized he was nervous.

A part of me liked to see Henry uncomfortable, liked to push his buttons in the way he pushed mine. So, naturally,

I did just that.

I started to read a random page out loud, but soon came to the understanding I'd stumbled into a sex scene that was more than graphic.

"Oh my God, stop. Just stop..." Henry cried, covering his face with his hands.

I lowered my voice, making it dark and gruff, keeping an absolute straight face when I got the spicy bits, drawing out the groans and sounds if only to agitate Henry because I found it endearing how he blushed, how he tried to hide the obvious tent in his sweatpants—those things hide nothing—until I was certain I had him on the brink of madness.

"You are insufferable," he groaned in defeat. "An absolute menace."

"Well, if that's the case, I think that's enough bedtime stories for tonight, don't you?" I breathed out as I tossed the book on my nightstand, before sliding back to my side of the bed.

Henry shifted from his position on top of the covers, to underneath, cursing under his breath. "And you say I'm the one who's infuriating," he murmured.

This time I did laugh.

Henry shut the light off, and settled on

his side of the bed, our breathing the only sound in the air.

We must have lain there in that bed for nearly twenty minutes, neither of us ready to fall asleep.

I noticed the shift in Henry's breathing as he tugged the covers over to his side, and instinctively, I moved toward him, giving up the fight. I cautiously slid my arm over his hip and gently tugged him against me. To my surprise, he didn't fight my touch, but instead relaxed into my hold, his breaths shaky.

"You are cold," I said, sliding my leg between his, pulling him back against my warmth.

"I mean, we are in the woods... It gets cold out here..." he murmured. He shifted in my arms as I fought the desire to let my fingers stroke his bare skin, trace lines over his soft edges.

To let my hands wander along the waistband and over his covered...

Henry sighed, turning in my grasp so that he was chest to chest with me. I could see him in the darkness, the only light that of the lanterns outside casting a faint fiery silhouette on him.

"Grayson... I..." His voice was soft,

barely a whisper. Then, I felt the faintest touch on my hip. A familiar warm palm rested against my exposed skin, and a sigh of relief escaped him.

"We don't have to do anything you don't want to do, Henry. I need..." I sighed in defeat of my own. "I need you to know that, okay?" I whispered, even though there was no need.

Henry pulled himself closer. I could feel his hardness against me, spurring me into arousal once more.

"Okay," Henry whispered.

Just as I thought this would end the way it usually did—with Henry getting jumpy and fleeing the scene, I was surprised.

Henry leaned in and *kissed me.*

But this kiss was different than the one we'd shared earlier, in the woods.

That had been a rush. Wild, unfettered, and brand new. But the way Henry kissed me now, as his hands slowly explored my stomach, my chest, my neck, and even my face, was something so much better.

His lips moved slowly against mine, his tongue slipping into my mouth with ease as he carefully caressed mine, sucking on my lower lip as he thrust himself against me, eliciting a deep, contented moan to bubble from my throat that I was powerless to stop.

I ran my hand over his perfect ass, gripping it as I thrust myself against his rigid hardness. I slid my hand beneath his waistband, just enough to feel the warmth of his skin against my palm.

A deep sigh escaped him as I let my fingers stroke his skin.

"You like that?" I breathed, slowly and as gently as possible tracing lines over his hip with my fingertips. "You like it when I touch you like this?" I asked as I ran my fingers over his heated skin.

Henry nodded as he kissed me again. He bit at my lower lip, sucking the flesh into his mouth as his clothed cock *throbbed* against mine.

"Yes," he breathed.

I trailed my hand over his stomach, letting my fingers brush against the trail of hair, teasing him. I meant what I'd said, and I didn't want to go any further without Henry's expressed consent.

"You can tell me to stop, if it's too much," I whispered into his mouth. "You don't owe me anything," I reminded him.

Though I hoped he wouldn't shut down what was happening between us, because it felt better than good.

It felt *right*... in a way it never felt with anyone else.

Henry's hand slid between us, and I half worried he was going to push me away, but instead, he leisurely slid his hand beneath the opening in my boxers, gripping my aching cock in his palm, squeezing just the slightest, and I shuddered with ecstasy.

The touch, *his* touch, was overwhelming.

"Henry," I groaned into his mouth.

"I don't want you to stop," he whispered, his thumb brushing my wet slit, spreading my precum over my swollen head.

"I just..." he breathed against me, his words full of hope, fear, and promise.

"What is it?" I asked, kissing him again. "You can tell me."

"I haven't wanted anyone like I want you... in a long time," he whispered.

"Fuck, Henry..." I moaned in defeat.

Henry wrapped his hand around my shaft, his warm palm squeezing me rhythmically.

"I want you too, Henry," I whispered, letting my lips travel from his mouth to his jaw, his neck.

With his free hand, he grabbed my forearm, pushing me lower. It wasn't much of a push, and I found Henry's sizeable erection rather quickly. I let my fingers trace its length, marveling at the texture of his thickness, committing to memory the feel of his veins and the thickness of his shaft.

The sound that escaped his lips was something like a cry and a moan all at once. I ran my thumb across his wet slit, spreading it in the same way he did to me.

"Make... make me come... Grayson, I'm so..."

"You didn't say *please*," I said, my voice gravelly and dark, nipping at his lips.

Henry thrust himself against me greedily as he stroked my shaft, which was now fully out of its boxer prison. His hand wrapped tightly around my shaft and I ground myself against him, fucking his hand until the head of my leaking cock brushed against his rough palm.

Fucking hell, Henry likes to play dirty!

"Please, Grayson..." he moaned into my mouth.

I wanted to feel his skin against mine, but I also didn't want to ruin this perfect moment.

I quickened my pace as I stroked him, squeezing in intervals. His cock throbbed in my hands, swollen and thick, and I could only imagine how it would feel in my mouth, cutting off my airway.

Fuuuuck...

"Oh fuck, Grayson, I'm—"

I covered Henry's mouth with mine, knowing I was about to come too.

Henry collapsed into my kiss, his entire body melting as his hot, wet release coated my hand, sliding through my fingers. His cock pulsed in my grip, and I came with an unrelenting growl, thrusting myself against his hold as I spilled myself in his hand.

I kissed Henry with promise, with hope. We were both a hot and sticky mess, but it felt like everything was different, and a good different.

Like we'd finally crossed some invisible line and everything was going to change.

And as we lay there, in blissful post-orgasm ecstasy, tangled together, I had never felt such peace.

I only hoped that when we woke up tomorrow, that peace would still be there.

CHAPTER TWENTY-SEVEN

Henry

I CURLED INTO the warmth surrounding me, breathing in the faint scent of smoke mixed with an underlying lavender.

Grayson.

Immediately, the memories of the previous day, and night, came flooding back to me. How we'd woken up together just like this—tangled around one another like vines—and how scared I'd been because I *liked* how it felt.

The way his fingertips traced smooth lines along my skin, or how his leg fit perfectly in between mine.

A part of me still wanted to panic, to run to the shower and gather my feelings so I could convince myself I *didn't* feel anything.

But as I opened my eyes, only to catch Grayson staring at me with a look that only made my insides melt and my cock twitch, I found resistance absolutely futile.

"Good morning, gorgeous," Grayson drawled, his voice still a tad bit hazy from his slumber as he gently kissed me. His palm against my hip was warm, but it didn't wander. Instead, it stayed frozen in one place as if he was panicking, as if he too, was nervous.

But I suppose that was my fault.

Grayson had more than called me out on my flighty behavior, at the fact that the closer he got, the more I pulled away.

But I couldn't help it. The last person I let get close to me...

He cheated on me.

The entire time we were together.

I knew it was irrational to think just because I'd had one bad apple meant the whole orchard was bad, even with the fact it had been years at this point since we ended our engagement and broke up. But the whole experience changed me.

Putting myself out there, trying to find

someone else, even a rebound, just didn't sit right with me. I'd thought I loved my ex, and that was why I was so devastated, so affected.

But as I lay there wrapped in Grayson's warm arms, staring at his beautiful face, I wondered if I ever really knew love at all.

Because the way Grayson looked at me, the way he touched me... and the way he let his guard down around me... it was impossible *not* to fall in love with him.

The realization scared me, but it also invigorated me.

I leaned into his soft kiss, relishing in the taste of his tongue on mine, letting my hands travel over the solid surface of his chest, up his neck until my fingers tickled the edge of his hairline.

"Good morning," I breathed into his kiss.

My cock twitched as Grayson tugged me closer, thrusting his morning wood against mine with a deep groan.

Just as I contemplated a replay of the previous night, a knock sounded on the door, making me flush with fresh panic. In the daytime, the domes were like large windows, which meant whoever was at the door, could likely see us. My entire body rushed with heat as we broke apart, Grayson only smirking at me as he swung his legs out of the bed.

"I, uh... think I'm gonna hit the shower," I said, coughing, if only to try and dispel the insecurity I felt at the moment.

I stumbled out of bed awkwardly, thanks to the maddening erection that was more than disappointed that our morning interlude had been cut short. I wasted no time disrobing once I was behind the partition and the glass sanctity of the shower, turning on water. Though I opted for warm water only because it was rather cold in the dome. I'd barely had time to get adjusted to the warmth before the door opened to reveal a rather jaw-dropping vision of Grayson.

Completely naked.

My gaze dropped immediately from his gorgeous face to his dick, which he held in his hand, his thumb lazily stroking his head.

My gaze flashed up to his sexy eyes, to his smirk.

"Now, where were we before we were so rudely interrupted?" he said as he stepped into the shower with me.

I couldn't move.

For starters, the shower itself wasn't that big. Sure, it was big enough we both could fit, but we couldn't both be under the showerhead at the same time.

Not to mention, it was one thing to *touch* Grayson's dick, but it was quite another to see him stroking his own erection in front of me as he watched me with a lustful gaze that only made my cock throb.

Grayson must have read my silence as a lack of consent, because immediately his eyebrows furrowed, and he dropped his hand.

"Unless I just interrupted *you*," he said cautiously.

And that snapped me out of my daze for some reason. I hated to see Grayson disappointed, which didn't make sense to me at the time.

I took one slow step forward, then another, until I was chest to chest with him and his back was flat against the shower wall. The squeak of his flesh against the glass echoed in the small space.

I reached out, trailing my hand over

his hip as I stared at him, hoping he could understand.

I wanted Grayson.

More than I think I could comprehend at the time.

"You aren't interrupting me," I whispered, watching as the water fell down over his skin in crystal clear rivulets.

Grayson slid his hand between us, his gaze fixated on mine as he ran his thumb over my slit before stroking me slowly. My eyes fluttered shut of their own accord as I tried to choke down the moan forming in my throat. But it was no use. My head fell against Grayson's shoulder as my hips rocked forth and I thrust myself against his relentless hand, once more.

"Look at me," he said, his voice full of command, full of lust.

I opened my eyes, lifting my head as I did what he asked.

His amber eyes held me still, like a statue. The only sensation I was acutely aware of was the warm water slicing over my skin and the pulsing of my cock in his warm, wet hand.

My lips parted instinctively as I sucked in a breath, and Grayson *praised* me.

"You are so fucking beautiful," he breathed, releasing my cock.

I whined without thinking, missing the feeling of his hand wrapped around me.

"Such pretty eyes you have," he whispered, holding me still against him, our stiff cocks rubbing against one another. My head rolled back as his lips assaulted my neck, right over my erogenous zone.

I wrapped my hand around him, and he groaned, taking my lips with his.

"And these lips..." He groaned, breaking away to trace his fingers over my bottom lip, gently tugging at the flesh.

"I've been fantasizing about these lips for days," he said, biting at my bottom lip in a way that made my fucking knees *buckle.*

My cock throbbed and I couldn't help but grind myself against him. With the way he was touching me, the tone of his voice... I couldn't help my sudden *need.*

My desperation.

I needed Grayson. I needed his order, his lead. I needed him to set me free.

With a shaky breath, I took his finger and slowly placed it in my mouth, taking careful precision not to gag myself—after all, that would be embarrassing—and slowly rolled my tongue around his finger, licking the tip of his finger, and groaning in slight exaggeration.

Grayson reacted just as I had hoped, cursing as he thrust himself against me.

"Such a little brat too," he huffed as he set his hands on my hips and turned us around, backing me up against the wall of the shower, water splashing and running down his back now. The chill of the glass against my flesh was a welcome contrast to the heat between us.

Grayson placed his hands on my wrists, spreading my arms at my sides as he ground his wet, warm cock against me.

I gazed up at his dilated eyes, his lips still swollen from kissing me.

"Grayson, I—"

His expression softened and he removed one hand from my left wrist, instead, using it to trace gentle lines along my jaw.

"Yes, baby?" he murmured, and I think my soul left my body.

"I w... want..."

"Tell me what you want, Henry," he said, kissing my lips gently. "Tell me and I'll give it to you."

GRAYSON

There were a hundred things I wanted to say, but because I'm a damn idiot and socially awkward as fuck, not to mention I'd been perpetually single for five years, the words that flew out of my mouth were, "I need you to know I'm clean. Before, we do anything else." I squeaked.

Grayson smirked. "Is that what this is about? Because I can assure you my record is spotless."

"I just... I meant what I said last night. It's been a long time, and I... I should just stop right now, I—"

"Henry." Grayson's smooth voice pulled me like a magnet. "I meant what I said too. We don't have to do anything you don't want to do," he said as he gently let up from where he pinned me. His fingers slid softly through my wet hair.

His words settled all the panic inside of me.

Because I did want him.

I wanted him so bad, it hurt.

"I want this," I said as I kissed him, pulling his weight against me once more.

Between his kiss, his revelation, and his words, I was a goner.

And my cock was aching for release.

Which is probably why the next thing out of my mouth was shocking even to me, but I couldn't deny that Grayson made me braver.

"I want you, on your knees." I swallowed harshly, my gaze flashing to his as I focused on his amber eyes. I needed to look at him, or I was going to lose my nerve.

"W... with my dick in your mouth," I managed to get the last part out without passing out.

Grayson didn't miss a beat as he slid to the ground, taking my rock hard cock in his hand and making quite the show of licking off the precum that had formed on my head with his perfect, pink tongue.

Sweet lord, if he keeps this up I might not even make it into his mouth!

My legs shuddered as he took me in one movement to the back of his throat. A deep, unrelenting moan escaped me as my back arched off the shower walls, my hands seeking his wet, silky locks to grip, to ground myself. My eyelids fell closed as he rolled his tongue around my shaft, hollowing his cheeks, while I gripped his hair, pushing him down further, spurred on by ecstasy I didn't even know I possessed.

A part of me worried I was going to choke him, but before I could pull back, Grayson slid his hands up my thighs, grabbing my ass as he *pulled* me closer, until I could hear the faintest gag from him.

I came without warning, hard and fast, my legs buckling beneath me and the only thing keeping me standing was Grayson's deep groan as he *swallowed* me down.

I opened my eyes, hazily gazing down at him. The sight before me would have brought me to release if I had not already being in the midst of coming.

Grayson, naked before me, cock swollen and gleaming, his perfect pouty lips stuffed with my cock and my release *dripping* down his chin with saliva and shower water.

I eased my grip on his hair, trying to catch my breath. When he was finished, and I had started to soften, he stood, bringing me close for a rather sloppy, salty kiss.

I'd never tasted *myself* before, and certainly never on anyone else.

But I didn't hate it.

In fact, I found myself melting into his

arms against the wall, my hands sliding in his hair once more as our tongues tangoed together.

When we broke away, Grayson laughed as he grabbed the shower gel, lathering his hands together, instructing me to turn around once more. His hands felt so good as he lathered my body, and the hot steam was relaxing. I almost felt like I could just curl up in bed once more and fall asleep. But that wasn't on the itinerary.

"We're going to be late for the wine festival," I exclaimed as all my faculties returned to earth.

"Oh hush. *We* will not be late. Everyone else will just be early," Grayson teased, sudsing my hair with shampoo.

I tilted my head back, running my hands through to wash it out, turning around once more to look at him, and do the same to him.

Maybe it was his use of the word *we,* or maybe it was just that I was accustomed to self-sabotage, but with my emotions and boundaries all over the place with Grayson, I felt a sting of panic.

"Um, Grayson... can I... can I ask you something?" I said, working up the lather of the shower gel across his solid pecs.

"Anything," he said almost so softly, I barely heard him.

I got the feeling that Grayson wasn't the type to get soft and warm, and that made what I was going to ask all the more difficult. But I wasn't as quick to wear my heart on my sleeve, and I wasn't exactly a spontaneous, go-with-the-flow guy.

"Can we... can we just keep this... us... between us, for now?" I asked hesitantly, worried I was going to destroy this perfect moment.

But with my head back on right, I knew it was best to set firm boundaries now so my heart wouldn't be broken later.

I understood Grayson was attracted to me. Hell, he'd made that abundantly clear by that point, and I was more than open to exploring what was happening between us, but until I had a firm grip on *my* feelings, I wanted to keep things private.

Relationships are between the people *in* the relationship, after all, and when things don't work out, or something happens, it's a lot easier to control the damage.

I'd learned that the last time.

Something shifted in Grayson's eyes,

but before I could discern what it was, he grinned that sexy Grayson grin, and nodded. "Of course," he said, switching me shower spots so he could rinse off.

I smiled in return, exiting the shower and grabbing my towel, feeling the best I'd felt in a long time.

Maybe this weekend wouldn't be so bad after all.

CHAPTER TWENTY-EIGHT

Henry

I TOASTED MIA with a glass of Rosé, some of it slightly sloshing out of my glass.

Grayson was animatedly telling a story about some weekend with his sister where they both ended up lost in a vineyard, the whole group roaring with laughter.

I watched him with drink-infused eyes, and my heart raced. Everywhere he went, he commanded attention, exuded authority.

I'd never been with anyone like him and that was as thrilling as it was scary. Because outside of the bubble Grayson and I had somehow built, I could see him the way everyone else did. And I could see how drastically different we were. But there was a spark within me that continuously burned, reminding me that the Grayson everyone else saw, wasn't the *real* Grayson.

Just like the me everyone else saw, wasn't the *real* me.

That spark, only made me want him more. It made me want to push and pull him, only to come undone under his command in private, pushed to my own limits. I wanted the Grayson who opened up to me, who was gentle and sweet when it mattered the most.

I wanted the sexy GQ model man who knew how to get me off with a *mere look.*

I wasn't one to drink usually, and I didn't think *tasting* would get me so off my rocker. The world was spinning, and the music was playing from the live band, and the sun was shining.

For the first time in what felt like forever, I felt *alive.*

As Grayson wrapped up his story, we all headed to the courtyard of the resort itself. Paved in stone with tents spread all across the field, it was a sight to behold.

GRAYSON

The resort was packed. With the wine festival being one of the biggest events of the year, apparently.

Thankfully, Giselle and her future husband had taken care of everything. I'd never had the chance to be on an exclusive, all paid vacation before, and though I'd offered to pay for my dome, Mia and Giselle thwarted my offering every chance I brought it up. After the fire the first night, I stopped, if only because Mia was getting exasperated at my insistence.

We all traipsed over to the picnic table in the center of the stone courtyard, the only one that was visibly empty due to the *reserved* sign on it. The girls threw down their purses in a flash as their dates settled with the boxes of the wine purchases everyone had made. "Come dance with me!" Mia said, tugging on Giselle's arm.

"I'll dance with you," I said, sweeping in to grab my sister as Giselle tumbled back into Aaron with a giggle.

"Come on, you lush," I teased as I hooked my arm in hers, pulling her up toward the dance floor.

"We'll be right behind you!" Julie called

out.

When we finally reached the dance floor, my sister seemed to have forgotten all about her friend.

I spun her around and she laughed, throwing her head back in joy.

"Are you having a good time?" I asked.

Mia's smile was bright. "The best time. How about you?"

I couldn't help but return her smile genuinely.

"I can't remember the last time I had this much fun," I said as I spun her out and then back in to my arms.

And for the first time in my life, it felt like the sky was the limit.

CHAPTER TWENTY-NINE

Grayson

THE RESORT WAS crawling with people, but as far as I was concerned there was only one person I was focused on.

My sister and her friends continued to drink and converse, the sun beating down on us and everyone within the courtyard. I watched as Henry spun his sister around the dance floor, smiling like he didn't have a care in the world.

I liked seeing this side of him—even if it was because of the several glasses of wine we'd been *tasting*.

I knew somewhere deep beneath the surface, this was who Henry was. He just needed someone to remind him.

"Excuse me," I said to no one in particular, as I made my way through the crowd toward the dance floor.

"Wait for me, Gray!" Julie crooned behind me, but I wasn't concerned about her.

I wasn't concerned about anyone except the fine specimen in front of me, who was lighting up the damn room. I saw the way the women on the floor were looking at him, and even some of the guys at the picnic tables I passed.

Possession swelled inside of me.

Mine.

That one is all mine.

"Sorry to interrupt," I drawled as I approached a pink-cheeked Mia, who almost instantly backed away from her brother.

Up close together, the family resemblance was obvious. They both had the same eyes, the same perfect bone structure. But the dark hair and eyes on Henry were much more sultry than the dark hair and blue eyes his sister sported, not to mention his perfect, luscious lips.

Lips that I want to taste over and over again.

Lips that I want wrapped around my

cock right about now.

"Oh, it's fine, Gray," Mia said with a hiccup, followed by a giggle.

Something sparkled in Henry's eyes as he crossed his arms, his black polo making his golden tan stand out all the more.

"My dance card is full," he said brattily, turning away from me. But I could see the hint of a smirk on his lips.

So, Henry wants to play.

"Perhaps you can make an exception," I whispered in his ear, shifting just so he could feel my arousal against his thigh.

As expected, his eyes widened, flashing to mine, filled with heat.

The music was loud, and Henry looked back at his sister, who was now dancing with Giselle and Julie in a circle, the three of them laughing like little kids.

I slid my hand around Henry's hip, pulling him toward me once more. The band struck up their next chords, something about she'd tell them what she really, really wanted... a melody and words that were achingly familiar, but I couldn't quite place. The bass was thick, and it was some semi-dark electronic beat that sounded more like a heartbeat than a song. The woman crooned huskily.

Henry swayed his hips back and forth to the music, moving in tandem as I pulled myself closer, acutely aware that everyone could see us.

But I didn't care. I wanted them to see us. I wanted everybody in fucking Brideshead to see what was mine.

"Everyone calls you Gray," he murmured. "Everyone but me."

I let out a dark chuckle.

"Is that what you want me to call you? Gray?" he asked hazily.

I hooked his chin under my knuckle, forcing him to look up at me. In his eyes, I could see a heat that was unmatched by any sun, any flame. I liked the sound of my name on his tongue, no matter how he said it. But something about the way he used my nickname, caused every nerve in my body to short circuit.

"You can call me whatever you want, baby," I whispered drunkenly as I pressed my lips to his.

To his own inebriation, Henry did not fight me. Instead, he melted against me like butter, groaning into my mouth, making my already hard cock twitch with anticipation.

"Gray..." he groaned my name, swinging his hips to the music, his dark eyes flashing at me with lustful haze.

"Yes, baby?" I responded breathlessly.

"Is it hot in here, or is it just me?" he asked, his cheeks red with heat.

"Need some air?" I asked, running my hands through his hair, feeling the heat of his flush.

Henry nodded as my fingers traced over his jaw, over his pout.

"Follow me," I commanded, squeezing his hand as I pulled him away from the dance floor.

"Where are we going?" he asked breathlessly.

I led him through the winding stone pathway, away from the noise, away from the drunken patrons and our wedding party.

Until I found just the place.

The underpass was much cooler, being in the shade, and it was also less populated. I pulled Henry to the side, into a darkened alcove, surrounded by potted plants and trees.

Henry's breathing was rapid, his cheeks still flushed.

"Gray—"

Before he could get the rest of the words out, desire took over, and I shoved him up against the stone arch.

"Do you have any idea how fucking hot you were up there? How many people were undressing you with their fucking eyeballs?" I nipped.

Henry ran a hand through his disheveled hair.

"Me?"

"Yes, you," I said as I took his face in my hands.

"Does that bother you?" he asked, his lips parted just enough to draw my attention.

Fuck, his mouth was so god damn perfect.

"You are *mine*," I said, gripping his hips as I thrust myself against him. "I don't like anyone else thinking they can have you," I breathed.

"I don't want anyone else," Henry said hopelessly.

"Show me," I growled.

Henry snapped my buttons like a damn powder keg, picking up exactly what I was throwing down.

"What if... what if we get caught?"

Well, that wasn't a no.

"You'll just have to be quiet then, won't you, baby?"

Henry slid his hand in between the slit in my boxers, his thumb brushing over my head swiftly. He kept his gaze trained on mine as I watched him slide down my legs to the ground.

I reached out, threading my fingers through his hair, licking my lips as I watched him take me into his mouth.

His tongue rolled around me and he lurched forward on his knees, forcing me into the back of his throat with a deep groan.

"Fuck," I cursed as his warm mouth cradled me. I tightened my fingers in his hair.

"You like that?" I asked, my voice dark and gravelly, gripping his hair and holding him to me, not giving him the chance to speak. But his grunts and groans were enough of a confirmation, as was the obvious bulge in his pants.

"What was that?" I asked, pulling him off of me so I could get a good glimpse at him. His perfect pout was swollen from kissing and sucking me, and his pupils were dilated beyond belief. He was the prettiest thing I'd ever seen.

"Yes," Henry breathed.

"Show me. Show me how much you want this cock," I spat, my words full of command, jealousy, and desire.

Make me yours, baby.

Henry didn't miss a beat as he took me down once more, sucking, licking, and rolling his tongue, deep, unrelenting groans of satisfaction emanating from his throat, vibrating through my cock.

"Fuck, Henry!" I cried, forgetting all about being quiet.

I didn't care if anyone saw us.

I wanted them to see.

Wanted everyone to know Henry was mine, and I was his.

I thought Henry swallowed every drop of me, because all my senses disappeared the moment I came, erupting in his throat like a fountain.

When I pulled him up from his knees, intent on buttoning my pants, Henry surprised me by going in for a sloppy, wet kiss, his mouth full of my load.

I fumbled with my pants as Henry rubbed his hardness against me, unloading my salty release into my mouth.

God, he is perfect.

Like the gracious man I was, I accepted it without hesitation, swallowing it like a champ.

Henry's kiss was unhinged. The slightest gasp of ecstasy escaped him, and I knew.

He fell against me, into our heat-filled kiss, an absolute mess.

We were both an absolute mess.

But in that space of disaster we were a perfect storm. Henry was rumbling, terrifying thunder, and I was bright, electrical lightning. An electric, perfect match.

I pulled away, taking in the sight of him in all his glory.

"Fuck, that was hot," I murmured, sliding my hand over his ass and cupping his cheek in my palm with a squeeze.

"Yeah, you are," he whispered back.

The music carried above us, and I was aware we needed to get back to the group. But I didn't care about the wine festival or listening to another one of Riley's dumb student stories.

A lazy grin spread on my face at his words, his genuine praise.

Fuck, I am.

I only cared about one thing.

"Mine," I whispered, kissing him gently.

"What?" Henry's voice was so soft I barely heard him.

"You're mine," I repeated. "And you're pretty hot too." I teased.

Henry looked up at me with glassy eyes. "You mean it?" he asked, his voice shaky.

I nodded, sliding my hand through his hair, gripping the strands once more and pulling his mouth to mine, my gaze falling on his. The world was a blur as I answered.

"Absolutely, baby."

CHAPTER THIRTY

Grayson

THE SUN SHONE through the dome like the Heavens were parting or something. Gold, bright, and far too early for my liking.

I blinked furiously, filtering the light. My head was pounding, my stomach empty as all hell, grumbling away.

I rubbed my eyes and sat up, the covers falling off of me. My gaze traveled to Henry, who was laying flat on his stomach, the covers barely covering him, his bare, pale ass on full display.

For a moment, I felt at peace, watching the rise and fall of his back, until I felt the urge to pee. Throwing off the covers, I swung my legs out of bed, my cock bristling from the friction of the sheet.

Head pounding, and half-dazed, I made my way to the bathroom, when I realized that I was also naked.

Panic laced through me as I tried to recall the prior night's events, but everything was a blur.

A wine-filled blur, and I couldn't remember anything after a karaoke-infused dinner at *Lovers Lodge,* the main bar that was open for the after-events of the festival.

I remembered arriving with Henry and everyone else, but I had no idea *how* we got back to the dome, or if we...

"Oh fuck," Henry's voice alerted me as he called out, "Grayson!"

I finished my business, heading back to the main room, to see Henry looked as panicked as I felt.

His gaze settled on me, and I stood there before him, feeling the most judged I have ever felt in my life.

What... what happened?" Henry asked, his voice shaky, and all I could do was shake my head nervously.

"I... I don't know," I said honestly. But that was apparently the wrong thing to say, because Henry's eyes widened.

"What do you mean you don't know?"

"I don't... uh... remember. Do you?" I asked, frozen in place.

Henry's eyebrows furrowed with concern, and I could see his breathing increase.

"No," he said, his voice laced with anxiety.

"All I remember is singing karaoke, and dancing..." He ran a hand through his disheveled hair, swallowing harshly. And then Henry said the quiet part out loud, and that changed everything.

"Oh my God, did we..." His voice elevated, the panic more than evident.

This was not how I wanted things to happen, if they were going to happen at all.

The fact I couldn't remember did not bode well. Henry deserved more from me.

I took a step closer toward Henry, who was sitting in bed now, breathing rapidly. I reached out for him, if only to soothe his panic, and perhaps my own. His gaze flashed at me as he pulled away, breaking my heart.

No no no no...

"Grayson, answer me..." he said, his

voice and his body shaking.

"I told you, I don't know. Everything is a blur. I—"

A knock sounded on the door, and Henry shook his head, throwing his legs out of bed with full force.

"I need a shower. Don't come after me," he said solidly. My shoulders fell in defeat as I watched him walk away, and the entire world felt like it was crumbling.

How could I have been so fucking stupid?

Because I was drunk.

As I surveyed the clothes strewn across the room, I picked up my underwear from the edge of the bed.

The answer was more than obvious. It wouldn't be the first time I got drunk and took someone to bed, but Henry wasn't like everyone else. He was different. Delicate, even.

And I'd just signed a one way ticket to destroying the foundation of something beautiful, something epic.

"The one good thing to happen to me in years, and I fuck it up. Good job, Gray," I said to myself, sighing in defeat as I headed to the door. The Breakfast cart was sitting at my doorstep, with an itinerary, but no annoying Cam to be found.

Even the staff knows I'm a fucking idiot.

I pulled the cart in, grabbing the itinerary and scanning the activities for the day. My sister had planned a morning hike to the Brideshead Waterfall, complete with waterfall side dining for lunch, and a formal dinner at *Wildfyre,* a reservation only restaurant between our glampgrounds and the Brideshead Resort's main lodge.

My stomach rumbled with hunger, but when Henry came out of the shower, not even turning to look at me, or acknowledging me at all, I lost my appetite.

CHAPTER THIRTY-ONE

Grayson

THE HIKE TO the falls wasn't as bad as I thought it would be, but I wasn't the only one who was hungover and tired as hell. Leave it to my sister, who had a liver made of steel, to book a mid-morning hike the morning after we'd been drinking for the majority of a whole day.

I sucked down some more water from the cooler on site, trying not to be a total creeper, but I couldn't take my gaze off Henry. I'd contemplated trying to talk to him, to apologize and tell him I was sorry, that I didn't mean for anything to happen...

I still couldn't remember exactly what happened, but all signs pointed to the obvious.

We slept together, and I didn't even remember it.

I wanted to remember it. Wanted to recall the feel of his body pressed against mine. I wanted to remember the look on his face as I inched my way inside him. I wanted to remember the moment he called my name, shattering around me.

But there was nothing. Nothing where those perfect memories should be, and I hated it.

But what was worse, was that Henry wouldn't even look at me. Instead, he avoided me like the plague and had taken up social interaction with his sister and Julie instead.

The Brideshead Waterfall raged behind me, a force of nature. It was beautiful, and the moment itself a stunning one, but I couldn't enjoy it because I wished I could be spending it with Henry by my side.

"Henry giving you the cold shoulder over your drunk makeout?" Giselle asked quietly.

"What?" I nearly jumped five feet off

the ground.

"Last night? The festival? You two could barely keep your lips off one another," she said with a smirk.

"I... don't remember."

"That sucks," she said taking a drink of her own water.

"Henry's such a reserved person to begin with. You, on the other hand..." She crossed her arms, nodding toward him and Mia who were laughing about something Julie said as she animatedly moved her hands.

"Drunk or sober, you're a total diva," she teased.

"I am not a diva," I snapped.

"You are the Susan Lucci of Jasper Springs, Gray. Dramatic as fuck."

I scowled. "Am not."

"All I'm saying is maybe you could learn a thing or two from Henry about slowing down."

My sister had no idea how right she was, and I despised that.

"Yeah, well, it was just a drunk kiss, right. Not like it means anything," I said.

Giselle pursed her lips. "It's okay to not be okay, Gray. We've all been there." Her words were sincere, but they only made me feel angrier. Worse.

"This isn't my first rodeo, Giselle," I growled, turning around to leave, running right into to object of my desire.

Henry's eyebrows furrowed, and I wondered how long he'd been standing there.

"Henry," I said softly, and he pushed past me.

"Excuse me," he said as he headed for the cooler, breaking my heart once more.

But perhaps I deserved such things.

Susan Lucci, and all.

CHAPTER THIRTY-TWO

Grayson

AFTER A DINNER fit for a king, Riley and Aaron decided to hit the billiards. Even Henry didn't protest, which was probably a testament to his mood.

"Aren't you playing, Gray?" Julie asked as she chalked up her stick.

I shook my head. They'd divided into teams. Boys against girls. Henry's gaze caught mine, making me feel all the more aware of how shitty I actually felt.

"No," I said, shaking off his judgmental stare. "I'm, uh, going to go for a walk, let this food settle a bit," I said with a fake smile.

Julie nodded. "Cool. We'll be here!"

I turned on my heel, heading out into the air-conditioned hall. I wandered aimlessly through the main lodge, toward *Reception*, a small bar-restaurant that served pretty much only bar food and drinks, when I heard someone call my name.

"Grayson Sanderson!" The voice was as charismatic as ever, and I didn't even have to look to know who it belonged to.

I turned slowly to see Cody, my ex.

I froze in place as I took in the sight of him. It'd been years since our affair, but he didn't look any different, save for some lines and wrinkles around his eyes.

"Cody," I said in the flattest voice possible.

After all, the man was responsible for forcing my coming out, and our drunken tryst had become a badge of dishonor, casting my family as a main source of drama and gossip for weeks.

I thought we were doing the right thing, keeping our affair a secret. After all, no one needed to know our business but us, right?

I thought I loved him at the time, despite everything, and that what were doing was just.

But as I looked at him in the light of *Reception,* I realized I never really loved him.

I was willing to take whatever I could get because I didn't think I deserved anything better than shadows and secrecy.

Which made me think about Henry.

We'd promised to keep whatever was happening between us a secret, but I'd slipped up. Maybe I did it on purpose.

Maybe I wanted everyone to know I was absolutely head over heels for Henry.

I'd never felt so strongly for another man in my thirty-eight years of life.

"What are you doing all the way up in these parts?" Cody asked, sipping a glass of whiskey. He motioned for me to sit, and I did.

"Giselle is getting married," I said evenly, testing the waters.

"I heard. We RSVP'd you know. The fam and I."

I nodded as a waiter came over to our table.

"Can I get you another, sir?" he asked, nodding to Cody's drink.

"Sure. And my friend here will have..."

Cody raised an eyebrow.

"Oh that's not necessary, I—"

"It's a drink, Gray. Not a marriage proposal," Cody teased.

I debated what the right thing to do was, but I'd never been the best at making *good* decisions.

If I was going to go down in flames, why not let the whole town see I was on fire?

"I'll just have a martini, dry—"

"Extra olives?" Cody said, grinning wickedly.

I nodded politely at the waiter, wishing he was someone else. A hotter waiter, with dark eyes, and sinful lips, and a heart of gold.

"You know what, scratch that. I'll have a glass of the Kendall reserve, thanks," I said, feeling more than agitated at Cody's nonchalance. The waiter left, and I shifted uncomfortably in the wooden chair.

"Am I that predictable?" I asked, leaning back in my chair.

"You have high standards. Nothing wrong with that. You know what you like."

"Anyway, Giselle thought it would be a good *bonding* experience to bring the party up here to spend the weekend glamping. Well, the party plus some friends," I said quickly, acutely aware it sounded like I'd come alone. Why I cared what this asshole thought was beyond my comprehension at the time.

"Glamping? That sounds like the gayest shit ever," Cody drawled, leaning forward in his chair, bringing himself closer to me.

Once upon a time, I thought Cody was *it*. His preppy style, his bad boy charm.

I could more than see why my sister always talked about him when they were together, and after we started hooking up, I could more than see his appeal.

But as I sat there, talking to him, sharing a drink, I saw him for what he truly was.

A fuckboy.

And I had no time for fuckboys, not anymore.

I only had time for one person. One person, who I needed to tell how I felt.

"I need to go," I said as I stood up, and Cody did too.

"Always on the run, Gray. You haven't changed at all," Cody said as he pulled me in for a hug.

I accepted, if only because it was a polite gesture, and that's where I went wrong.

I'd misjudged Cody's intentions, apparently. Because when he pulled away from the hug, he pulled me in closer, and planted a wet, drunken kiss on my lips.

"Just like old times," he drawled sourly into my mouth.

CHAPTER THIRTY-THREE

Henry

I WATCHED GRAYSON leave the billiards, feeling like a complete and utter failure of a human being.

All day I'd ransacked my brain, trying to find even a shred of memory of what had happened between us, but there was nothing. I hadn't truly blacked out from drinking since my freshman year of college, in which my sister had to take my ass home.

And after that, I swore I'd never get black out drunk again, knowing the position I put myself in.

But I'd had a good time, up until my memory faded to black. The things I could remember—singing karaoke with Mia, Julie, and Grayson, sucking Grayson off underneath the underpass, tasting all the wine, dancing with my sister—I had meant what I said to Mia. I couldn't remember the last time I had so much fun.

I hated that I couldn't remember what had happened between us.

Casual sex wasn't something I did.

But I knew, despite having no memory of it, that was exactly what happened.

We fucked.

There was a sliver of a chance that we might have just passed out, but I *could* remember making out with Grayson, among other things, so the leap was only logical.

And I'd be lying if I said I *didn't* want to be fucked by Grayson. Or that I didn't think about fucking him. Which was certainly a new development for me, being as I'd never topped anyone before.

But it wasn't the ninety-nine point nine chance we had sex that bothered me. What bothered me was that I had been careless with my heart, and with Grayson's.

I wanted to take my time with

GRAYSON

Grayson. I wanted to be sure he wasn't going to break my heart like my ex. I needed to *trust* him. I needed to know with absolute certainty that Grayson didn't just see me as a fun weekend, and was going to discard me the minute we got home. I needed to know Grayson saw me as more than just the younger brother of his sister's bestie, and I also didn't want things to be awkward after this weekend, with the wedding on the horizon and any other events I might see him at. After all, this weekend wouldn't last forever.

What was going to happen when we arrived home and went back to reality?

Would Grayson still want to be with me without all the romance and sophistication surrounding us?

When the reality wasn't all glamping tents and waterfall hikes and expensive wine?

I wanted more than anything to tune out the anxiety, the panic, and the negative thoughts that threatened to sour the best weekend I'd had in a long time. But I couldn't get my head out of my ass, and because of that, I watched Grayson leave, and I did nothing.

Mia nudged me from my internal prison. "Your turn," she said, her gaze soft, understanding.

I grabbed my stick, lining up my shot as I sucked in a deep breath.

Some things in life were simple. Like playing pool. The rules were understood, and there was a clear indication of what to expect when you played the game. I wished life was like that. Easy to understand, easy to play.

Instead, it was messy and chaotic. It was scary and thrilling, and beautiful and ugly all at once.

Crack!

The clacking of the balls sounded together as they dispersed, the eight ball going right in the corner pocket like I had hoped.

Giselle whistled in approval as Riley and Aaron high-fived one another.

"Damn, Henry, I wish my brother were here to see that. He's the best player when it comes to the game. I bet you could give him a run for his money."

Giselle said with a smile.

"I'd love to see that," Aaron said with a laugh. "Someone putting Gray in his place for once."

GRAYSON

My blood chilled, my face expressionless at the casual mention of the object of all my desires.

Their words only made me feel worse.

Giselle took her spot, as Riley reset the rack. Mia settled beside me.

"Did something happen? Between you two?" she asked gently.

"Oh something happened," I murmured. "But, neither of us can really remember *what.*"

Mia's eyes widened, her mouth forming an 'o'. "And that is a bad thing?" she asked cautiously.

I felt my shoulders loosen with defeat.

"I just... I don't want to be some casual... fling, Mia. I—" I ran my hand through my hair, feeling the heat of my skin as my words spilled out of me relentlessly. I was powerless to stop them.

"You like him," she said, her voice solid, matter of fact. It wasn't a question.

"Yeah, I do," I whispered, my voice shaky.

"So then tell him," she said as if it was the most obvious thing in the world. I sighed.

"I can't." I admitted.

"Why not? That man was pining after

you all fucking day, and you can't even see it, can you?" She huffed.

"What?"

"You are so thick sometimes, Henry. Not everyone is a liar and a cheat like—"

"I know that, Mia," I snapped.

"Do you? Because it looks to me like you're living in the past with a ghost instead of living in the moment with someone who is obviously crazy about you."

"It doesn't matter," I sighed, fidgeting with my stick. "I fucked everything up, anyway."

"Then fix it," she said, as Julie called her to take her turn.

I watched my sister line up her shot, her gaze flashing at me before she struck.

The balls scattered across the green in all directions, and hers slowly crawled to a stop, in the middle.

I passed my stick off to Riley, not wasting another moment. "I'll be back," I said, leaving it at that as I trotted off in the direction Grayson had disappeared.

Anxiety still flooded me, but now it was met with something else.

Hope.

I'd been so focused on the fact I'd

messed everything up, I hadn't even given a thought that maybe I *could* fix it. Apologize for my dumb behavior. Tell him I liked him.

Maybe even... loved him.

I stopped dead in my tracks as I set my gaze on him. He was standing up from a table, where he was with someone and they looked pretty chummy. The man moved to hug Grayson, wrapping his arms around him. Grayson wrapped his arms around the man, and then... and then he kissed him.

My heart shattered into a million pieces at the sight.

"Fucking knew it," I said, turning around on my heel, only to hear Grayson call out my name.

Tears prickled my eyes as I headed toward the exit, toward the transport concierge.

"Henry, wait," he called.

I held my sob in the entire ride back to the glamping tent, my fist balled as I felt like crumbling. Just as we arrived, the rain started to pour, and I ran from the transport to the front step as fast as I could to avoid getting soaked.

I threw open the door of the dome,

relishing in the silence of being alone and I let out a gut wrenching sob that was as desperate as it was painful.

"Fuck," I cried, slamming my fist against the domed windows. I tore away, headed for the shower, when the door opened, pulling my attention once more.

Grayson stood in the doorway, the lantern light casting a golden glow on him, his blue button down soaked, clinging to his perfect chest, his dark hair wet, hanging in his eyes like some Esquire Brand Mr. Darcy.

And I both hated and loved it all the same.

"I can't do this with you," I said, my heart beating so loud I thought it would echo in the room.

"Henry, please, it's not... it's not what it looks like," he said as he took a step closer.

Enraged with several years of pent up baggage, in his presence I came undone.

"Oh really, Grayson? You going to tell me he tripped and fell onto your perfect mouth, and you were giving him CPR?" I growled.

"He's... Cody's not important to me. Not anymore."

I let out a dark laugh. "Anymore, right."

"Henry, please, just listen to me!"

"Listen to you? Listen to what, your lies? You said I was *yours!*" I cried, my stomach turning in anguish.

"You promised!" I yelled, as several years worth of trauma unleashed itself on Grayson.

Grayson stepped forward, but I held my hand up to stop him. I worried if he got any closer, I might actually explode into a million pieces.

"Don't," I said shakily. "Just... leave me alone," I said through tears and sobs.

"Henry..."

"I mean it, Grayson," I said as I headed for the shower, not looking behind me. Because I knew if I did, I would see Grayson's heart breaking too.

And I'd know it was because of me.

CHAPTER THIRTY-FOUR

Grayson

THE MORNING WAS quiet. Too quiet.

I'd spent the night tossing and turning, my body cold from the chill in the air. Henry slept curled up on the edge of the bed, far away from me.

It had been poor timing that he'd show up the moment Cody decided to be... well, Cody.

I'd pushed him away, but the damage was done. Henry saw him kiss me, and he must have thought...

Well, it was more than apparent what he thought, because the tears running down his face were enough to cut me to the bone.

I'd pleaded with him to listen, but he wasn't capable of listening. Seeing Cody and I set off some trigger, something buried beneath Henry's charming, sweet exterior.

Perhaps it was the very trigger that had kept him with one foot out the door, this entire weekend.

Whoever had hurt him... I wanted to wring their fucking neck. For tarnishing this perfect man who deserved the world and made him think he wasn't enough.

He was worth more than gold.

I needed to make him understand that as far as I was concerned, there was no one else, and the moment I saw him crumble before me, his voice full of pain as he cried "you promised," I knew there would never be anyone else.

Because I was in love with Henry.

I was completely balls to the wall, head over heels, soap opera style in love with Henry.

He showered and dressed without a word, packing up his suitcase. After wine check, we were wrapping up the afternoon with spa appointments, and then we'd be leaving.

It would be time to head back to

reality.

A reality where Henry and I would part our ways.

Probably never to speak again, given everything that's happened.

"Cam's here," Henry said coolly, dragging his suitcase by the door.

"Right," I said, the tension between us palpable. There were so many things I wanted to say, but I couldn't find the words.

CHAPTER THIRTY-FIVE

Grayson

I CLOSED MY eyes, trying to enjoy movements of the masseuse who was massaging my temples, but it was no use.

"You are tense," she said. "Relax."

"That is the point of a spa, you know," Giselle murmured from beside me.

Aaron was not a fan of the spa, and instead had opted for a classic shave at the shop below, while my sister, Julie, Mia, and I all enjoyed a mid-morning facial.

"Yes, well, it's been a rough weekend," I nipped, not in the mood for my sister's prying antics.

"What part was rough?" Julie teased. "You looked like you were enjoying yourself to me."

I peered at Julie by opening one eye.

"I don't see how that is any of your business."

"Does this have anything to do with why you left pool early and never came back?" Mia asked, and I grumbled as the masseuse held my head still, chastising me.

"Relax!" she barked.

"That is damn near impossible," I said, getting up from my seat.

"Where you going?" the masseuse asked, obviously surprised at my gesture.

"To the Jacuzzi. To *relax*!" I snapped, turning on my heel and taking off for a lounge that wasn't full of gossiping bridesmaids and a bride-to-be.

I ended up in the men's spa, disrobing so that I could soak in the Jacuzzi alone for a moment and collect my thoughts. I'd just closed my eyes when I heard the door open.

"Oh, I didn't realize you were in here," Henry's voice was soft.

I opened my eyes, my gaze fixed on him, his fingers playing with the tie of his fluffy robe. He had the audacity to look hurt. As if I was the one who had ruined him.

As if the very sight of him didn't cause my heart to race.

"You don't have to leave," I said.

"Are you sure—"

"Stay," I said, my voice shaking. One word.

I wanted him to stay, and I wasn't just talking about his presence in the spa.

I wanted Henry to stay *with me*.

But I could barely get the words out before his stomach rumbled. I watched his cheeks flush as he twisted his lips.

"Hungry?" I asked.

"I, uh... haven't really had much of an appetite today," he said cautiously.

"You should eat something," I insisted.

Henry disrobed, peeking over his shoulder at me for a moment before sliding his spa sandals off. I watched as he slowly walked over to the Jacuzzi opposite my side. Away from me.

Part of me wanted to rise and join him, to pull him into my arms and tell him I was sorry.

I was sorry someone somewhere made him feel like he wasn't enough.

I was sorry for compromising us both the other night.

I was sorry for sitting down in the first place with Cody, thinking he had changed, because I had changed.

But most of all, I was sorry for whatever pain I had caused Henry, and I wanted to make it right.

I wanted to be the man to heal his wounds.

I wanted to love him the way he deserved to be loved.

But I said none of that, because the masseuse came in, setting her gaze on me with fury.

"Your time is up, Mr. Sanderson," she said, tapping her watch. The spa ran in fifteen-minute intervals, and I was well over my time.

"Understood," I said, rising from my pool, feeling the chill of the air from the shift in temperature. I grabbed my robe, tying it closed as I followed the woman out.

"Could you see that my friend in there, Henry, receives a charcuterie platter and a pastry assortment along with a selection of your finest teas and coffees, please," I said as I headed toward the locker room.

"And, please, put it on my tab," I ordered.

The woman smiled pleasantly. "Of course, Mr. Sanderson, will there be anything else?" she asked as I stopped at the door.

"Anything he wants, of course. Tell him it's been taken care of."

CHAPTER THIRTY-SIX

Henry

THE DRIVE HOME was thick with unsaid words. Grayson kept switching radio stations, until I finally relented, turning it off altogether. I supposed it was time to rip the band-aid off and address the elephant in the Porsche.

"I can't do this. This awkward silence. We need to talk."

"I couldn't agree more," Grayson said, not looking away from his attention on the road.

There was so much I wanted to say, but all I could settle on was, "I'm sorry I yelled at you."

Grayson's expression did not shift.

"Yes, well. Cody has that effect on people," he murmured.

"Is he your—"

"Was."

Hope dared to blossom in my heart, but I needed to get things out. I could not be distracted by slivers of hope.

"I'm sorry too," Grayson said softly as the GPS announced a turn.

I glanced at the map screen, reading the ETA. Thirty minutes.

I only had thirty minutes left with this man who I was certain was holding my heart hostage.

I wanted to tell him he couldn't have it.

My heart.

Me.

But the truth was, he had it the moment he looked up at me from the bathroom floor of M's Place. I just didn't know it then.

But before I could even speak the words out loud, Grayson continued.

"I never meant for any of this to happen... like this." He sighed. "I never intended to hurt you, Henry."

Panic laced through me at his words, hope fighting for a chance to breathe.

But it would not win. Not that day.

"I never wanted things to be awkward between us," I said, my heart in my throat. "Some friend I am, huh?" I said, blowing out a defeated breath as I looked out the window. I couldn't look at Grayson, knowing the blow was coming.

"Is that what we are? Friends?" Grayson asked warily.

I couldn't look at him, nor could I answer him. Not when I felt like the harsh truth of reality would smack me in the face.

"Because if that's all you see me as, Henry, that's... fine, but..."

I sat up in my seat, scooting to the edge as I waited for him to continue.

A notification popped up on the map screen, the electronic voice calling "Text from uncle Bob, would you like to hear?"

"No," Grayson said coolly, turning onto the main drag into Jasper Springs.

I'd be home in ten minutes.

"But I'd hoped maybe we could be more than that. More than friends, I mean."

The air fell silent.

Every nerve in my body stood at attention, that hope blossoming in my chest like a bad weed.

I wanted to be more than friends, too, but...

But I needed time. Everything had happened so fast, and...

"I can't," I said as he pulled up to the parking lot.

I wanted him to fight. To take my face in his hands and kiss me, like he had in the woods, and tell me I was a damn fool.

I wanted Grayson to rescue me from myself, but he wasn't capable of that.

I needed to rescue myself, first, from the ghosts that haunted me.

Grayson didn't do any of those things.

He only smiled softly, and said, "Okay. Just friends then."

I opened my door as Grayson got out, unlocking the trunk. I grabbed my suitcase as he tapped away at his phone absentmindedly.

"Thanks for... the ride," I said, turning to head down the hill to my apartment.

"Uh huh," he said as he leaned against his car in that graceful, seductive way that made my cock twitch.

I hoped I was doing the right thing, protecting Grayson.

Protecting myself.

CHAPTER THIRTY-SEVEN

Grayson

THE HOUSE WAS empty, as it always was at this time of day.

While I relished in the isolation, usually, this time it was not what I needed.

What I needed was Henry and his perfect mouth, his presence, his understanding.

How had everything become so complicated, so fast?

I knew the answer, but I didn't want to admit any of it. Or my part in it.

I wanted to blame Henry and his obvious baggage. I wanted to blame Henry and his push me, pull me, brat attitude.

But I knew Henry wasn't the *only* factor. I'd pushed, and pushed, but I hadn't told Henry the truth.

I'd hid the truth from myself by covering it up with steamy kisses, and tangled limbs, and drunk sex.

The truth was I was absolutely in love with Henry.

And he wanted to be *friends*.

The emptiness of the house echoed with my sob. I couldn't remember the last time I cried over a man, period.

But Henry wasn's *just* some casual fling.

I meant every word I said in that car.

I wanted more.

I wanted to lay in bed with Henry reading gay ghost porn, and I wanted to roast a million s'mores with him, and I wanted to watch him get all flustered trying new things.

I wanted to play push me, pull me until we both were so worked up we'd have to fight for dominance.

I wanted to dance with him at my sister's wedding, and kiss him under the stars until he couldn't breathe. I'd never felt like this about anyone.

I'd never fallen in love like *this*.

My phone rang, pulling me from my meltdown.

"You home yet?" Giselle asked when I answered, and I sighed, wiping my nose with the back of my hand as I tried to stuff down my sobs.

"Yeah," I said, my voice shaky.

"You okay, Gray? You sound upset."

She didn't know the half of it.

"I'm fine, sweetheart. You guys get home okay?" I asked, trying to change the subject to anything else so I didn't fall into deeper despair.

"Yeah, we just got in. Aaron is meeting up with some friends tonight. I was actually going to call up Drew and see if he wanted to hang out now that we're back, I was thinking M's Place? You can join if you want..." she said, her voice full of excitement.

Just for once, I wished I had the positivity my sister had. That I could just enjoy myself like she did, flitting from event to event like a butterfly.

I sighed, "Yeah, okay. See you there."

CHAPTER THIRTY-EIGHT

Grayson

MAYBE I WAS holding on to wishful thinking. Hoping that life would be like a romance novel, and I would show up to M's Place and sweep Henry off his feet. We'd kiss, and apologize for being stupid assholes, and live happily ever after.

But Henry wasn't there.

I stared at my martini, but I hadn't touched it, when Giselle bumped my shoulder. Drew—the famous Drew Axel who'd come back to Sweetewater and reconnected with my sister recently on his tour, and who was now dating her florist, of all people—and his beau were on their way.

"You haven't touched your martini," she said softly.

"Thought I wanted it, but I guess I'm not in the mood."

Giselle twisted her lips, and then she let out a bombshell.

"Did you know Henry was engaged before?" she asked.

My gaze shot up to hers, eyes widening. "What?"

"About five years ago," she said, stirring her drink.

I was floored. Henry never mentioned his ex, but I would have thought he would have at least mentioned being *engaged,* given our company, not to mention all the talk of weddings...

"No," I said dumbfounded. "I had no idea."

Suddenly, his being uncomfortable around the wedding party made a lot more sense. I closed my eyes as I realized I should have seen it. His fear of commitment, his apprehension to act on his attraction.

I can't.

Not I won't, I *can't.*

Because the person who hurt Henry

was someone he must have loved very, very much. Enough to want to spend the rest of his life with them.

"What happened?" I asked.

"Apparently, according to Mia, the guy had been cheating on him. From the get go."

"For five years?" I asked dumbfounded.

Giselle nodded. "Henry found out because he came home early one night."

I let out a shaky breath. "He found them together."

Giselle nodded. "Broke off the wedding the day after, and he's been a lone wolf ever since."

Henry's tear-streaked cheeks and the anguish on his face replayed in my brain.

You promised.

You said I was yours.

The words fell out of my mouth, vulnerable and full of emotion.

"He said... he said he just wanted to be friends," I breathed.

Giselle offered me a look that said, "Are you serious?"

"He's scared, Gray. Can you blame him?"

No, I couldn't. Not now, not when I knew *why*.

"I mean, anyone with eyeballs could see you two are crazy about one another. Last I checked, friends don't kiss each other the way you do, drunk or sober," she said raising her glass to me.

"Hell, Aaron doesn't even kiss me like that," she said with a laugh.

I blushed at her insinuation.

What the fuck was happening to me?

"A word of advice? One Sanderson to another?" she said, much more serious.

I sighed. Knowing my sister, I'd get the advice whether I said yes or no. So, of course, I said yes.

"He just needs to know you're not going to bail when things get hard."

"I'm not—"

"Not everything has to be Susan Lucci, Gray. Love isn't always trays of pastries and charcuterie or extravagant resorts. Sometimes it's just the little things."

"Like roasting a marshmallow," I said dumbly.

"Like dancing along to the Spice Girls," she said sweetly.

"Or reading gay ghost stories,"

My sister raised her eyebrow, but she didn't press me.

Drew and Taylor walked through the

door at that moment, Drew calling out for us, shattering the tense moment.

I knew what I had to do at that moment.

I'd been waiting for a prince charming of my own to rescue me, but what if I was the knight in shining armor?

CHAPTER THIRTY-NINE

Henry

I STOOD IN line with my sister, indecisive over what I was going to order for lunch.

It'd been nearly three days since I had gotten back from Brideshead. Three days, and a hundred unsent, deleted texts I couldn't find the courage to send.

I'd done everything I could, focusing on work, watching movies, I'd even started *running* on the outdoor trail with some of the other tenants from my building.

Nothing would erase Grayson Sanderson from my mind.

Which was probably why I leapt at the chance to grab something to eat with my sister. Even if only for an hour or two, I could focus on something that wasn't my royal fuckup of the century.

The first man to come along since my ex, and I'd completely ruined everything because of...

Well, because I couldn't fathom how anyone would want me, when I wasn't good enough for him.

I'd been so excited when he proposed, all those years ago.

At the idea of forever.

I thought our love was the things dreams were made of.

But I knew then, standing there in the cafe, that it was all me.

I saw what I wanted to see. I saw a young, attractive man who was friendly enough in public, but who always had to "work late" or attend some function I wasn't invited to.

I never saw the signs he was cheating, because I truly believed he loved me.

Because I loved him.

Or rather, I loved the idea of him. A fiancé, a husband. Maybe even a father. And all those dreams fell apart the minute the truth was revealed. He never wanted me. He never really wanted to get married, he told me that night. He was doing it because it was just what was expected when you'd been with someone a while, and I seemed like a nice enough guy.

I'd closed myself off after that, because I didn't want to be someone's number two option. But in doing so, I became so closed off that I didn't even consider the possibility that I could be someone else's number one priority.

Like I said, I have the worst fucking luck.

"What are you getting?" Mia asked.

"Probably the same thing I always get," I said as we moved up in line.

That's when it clicked.

I looked at the menu, remembering the day Grayson and I met up—so I could give him back his wallet, of all things. Because he'd left it at my house.

He'd teased me for keeping my order simple, and then nonchalantly shoved a cinnamon roll at me.

Offering me more than just a dessert.

He was offering me a chance to try something new. A chance to break the same cycle, the same rut I'd been stuck in.

Big changes, start with small ones.

A lost wallet.

A cinnamon roll.

A horseback ride.

A kiss.

I looked at the menu differently after that.

"You know what, I think I'm going to change it up this time," I said. "I'll have the caprese wrap. And a cinnamon roll. With a cafe mocha, please."

Mia shrugged. "I didn't think you liked cinnamon rolls. You always said they were too sweet."

A soft smile tugged at my lips. "People can change you know," I said, feeling the weight of my words, as I thought about all the ways I *had* changed, just in these last few weeks.

With Grayson.

We don't have to do anything you don't want to do, he had said.

Granted, when he said it I knew he meant sexually, but I realized at that moment as I placed my order, that his words went beyond the physical attraction we shared.

This dynamic, bold, commanding man who was a natural born leader was more willing to defer when it came to *me*.

That depends, will you let me lead?

His words reverberated in my brain.

I'd never once considered that I was topping from the bottom, but I realized I was.

I pushed and pulled at Grayson, unsure of my footing, of my feelings. But nothing in life was certain.

Nothing except the moment we had in front of us.

And all that truly mattered was how we spent those moments. I'd spent them worrying, talking myself in circles and telling myself I wasn't enough for Grayson, instead of *allowing* myself the pure joy and happiness I felt when I was with Grayson to rule me and my heart.

"Have you heard from Grayson at all?" Mia asked as she finished her order, walking over to the counter with me.

I shook my head, all the truth converging on me at once. I needed to fix this. I needed to apologize, and I needed to make things right.

Because I didn't want to keep repeating the same thing over and over again. I wanted things to be different.

I deserved the chance to love again. I deserved happily ever after.

"No, I, uh... I think I fucked up, Mia," I

said, grabbing my tray.

Mia blinked at me in confusion. "What? What do you mean?"

"I've been a fucking asshole to Grayson..."

Mia's gaze softened as she said, "Ahhhhh."

"Fuck," I cursed.

Mia blinked again. "You don't usually curse," she said as we took our seats.

"I know," I said, taking a sip of my mocha latte. I'd never had one before, but it tasted pretty good.

New things.

New experiences.

New is not a bad thing.

"I just don't know how I'm going to fix it, but I need to."

"Just call him." She shrugged. "You think too much," she nipped.

"What if... what if I call him and he wants nothing to do with me? What if I blew it?" I asked, biting my lip.

Mia popped a tater tot in her mouth. "What if you haven't? What if your prince charming is waiting for you to come to your senses?" she said with a grin. A shit-eating grin.

"You know something I don't, Mia?" I

asked, narrowing my gaze at her.

Mia puckered her lips, her grin mischievous. "Only thing I know is Grayson leaves work in about an hour. He should be home by five o'clock."

"And how do you know that?" I asked, a plan already forming in my brain.

"That's not important," she said, plopping another tater tot in her mouth as I slid my phone out of my pocket.

My fingers hovered over the letters of my keyboard nervously. I pushed the nerves down though, knowing they'd always be there. Until maybe, one day they wouldn't be.

New things, Henry.

New things equal new results.

Are you free tonight to meet up for some coffee?

I sent the text, letting out a deep breath as I did so. I expected to wait a while, after all it had been days since I heard from him.

But he messaged me back almost instantly.

Absolutely.

CHAPTER FORTY

Henry

I WAITED PATIENTLY with my coffee, watching the door. When Grayson appeared, panic spread instantly. But I shoved it down for the moment, focusing on the tall, hot as hell man in front of me, dressed in a nice suit.

I preferred the dressed down version of Grayson, but he looked like a damn wet dream in a suit.

My cock voiced our opinion rather loudly and I crossed my legs.

"You rang," Grayson said as he sat down, folding his hands in his lap.

"Do you want to get a coffee first?" I

asked, nodding to the counter. There was no line.

"Are you offering to buy me a coffee, Henry?" he teased.

"I am," I said nonchalantly.

"Well, in that case, I shall keep it simple," he said as he rose from his seat, and I followed him to the counter.

"I'll have a flat white, please," he drawled, his tone smooth like the cream that would no doubt grace the top of his latte.

"I tried something new today," I said, breaking the ice as they handed him his coffee.

"Really?" Grayson asked, sipping his drink.

"I thought about something you said." I shrugged, leading us back to the table.

Grayson sat gracefully, crossing his legs and I sat beside him. He cast me a wary glance, but he did not move.

"What did I say?"

"Do you remember when we first came here? I came to give you your wallet back—"

"Ah, yes. How could I forget the beginning of our... friendship," he said cautiously, but I could see the spark in his eyes. The longing.

Maybe we could be more.

I want to be more.

"You teased me, about my *simple* order. Then you bought me a cinnamon roll."

"Yes, well, dessert is the best part of a meal."

"Change is hard for me, Gray."

I didn't miss the way his entire body relaxed, the way his shoulders fell, his eyes watered at the mention of his nickname.

The next words out of my mouth were the hardest, but I knew if I didn't say them, I'd regret it.

"But I know change is a lot easier with you."

Grayson let out a breath, taking another sip of his coffee.

"I don't like cinnamon rolls, though," I said, clearing my throat.

Grayson smiled wickedly. "Then we will simply find you a suitable replacement."

I focused my gaze on him, fully aware we weren't talking about dessert anymore. Which should have scared me but... it didn't.

Because I trusted Grayson.

I trusted him with my whole heart.

"Well, I mean... there is one dessert, I really like," I said, feeling a blush creep on my cheeks.

"What is that?" Grayson said, his fingers stroking the sides of his cup in slow motion. He shifted his legs, fidgeting in his seat as he cleared his throat.

At the risk of sounding like an absolute idiot, the words fell out of my mouth. "A good cup of coffee," I said as I raised my cup.

Grayson raised his in repose. "You deserve the best coffee there is, Henry."

"I already have the best coffee there is."

CHAPTER FORTY-ONE

Henry

THE CAR WAS silent and heavy with tension as Grayson turned it off.

It was now or never.

Six little words.

Six words that would bring about a change I knew there would be no going back from.

"Do you want to come in?" I asked, my words loud in the space between us.

Grayson looked at me skeptically, biting his lip. "Do you want me to?" he asked, his gaze full of hope.

Full of love.

I nodded. "Yes. I do."

Grayson opened the door without

saying a word, and I did the same. He walked me to my apartment, which felt like an eternity. We stood on my front step, and I fumbled with my keys, my nerves getting the best of me.

"Hey," he said, holding his hand over mine. "Nothing has to happen..."

I opened the door, his fingers sliding around my wrist as I turned the key. I gazed up at him, and I'd never been so sure of anything as I was in that moment that I loved him.

That as long as I had him, I could make it through anything. Even the hard, uncomfortable moments.

"I love you," I said, the words heavy in the air.

I opened the door, the both of us looking into the darkness.

Into the realm of uncertainty.

"I love you, and I want you to stay. I want you to stay with *me.* I know I won't always say the right thing, or do the right thing, and I'm not some polished, perfect—"

Grayson pulled me close, capturing my lips with his and we stumbled in the door. I kicked it closed as I fought to wrestle my arms around his neck, pulling him closer against me, needing his kiss, his tongue, his touch.

All of it.

I needed *him.*

"Oh, Henry," he whispered my name like it was a prayer, his lips and tongue caressing mine with so much passion, I felt like I would catch fire and spontaneously combust.

"I love you too," he whispered. "I've wanted to hear you say that for so long," he murmured, his hands traveling down my shirt, resting on the waistband of my jeans.

I could feel his hardness against my own, and the euphoria of his words shattered the last bit of my armor.

"But I didn't want to scare you away..."

I felt lighter, better, having said them. The truth couldn't hurt me anymore.

It could only make way for something better. Something brighter.

Because when Grayson said those words, *I love you, Henry,* I felt it.

I felt the truth, the weight of them, and in his eyes I could see he truly meant it.

He loved me.

Despite everything that had transpired, everything we'd done, everything I'd said...

This man loved me.

"You're mine," he whispered.

"Promise?" I asked, my fingers sliding up beneath his shirt.

Grayson picked me up, my body reacting instinctively to his hold as I wrapped my legs around his waist. His hands cradled my ass as he carried me to the couch, all but throwing me down on it.

I leaned back, taking in the sight of him, his vivid erection practically punching through his pants, dark hair falling in his eyes, lips swollen from kissing me. He grabbed himself, licking his lips and my cock twitched with anticipation.

"Promise," he said, his voice dark and gravelly, removing his pants.

I quickly hurried to free my own cock, my gaze trained on him as he slowly undid each button on his shirt until he was standing before me.

God, he was sexy as fuck.

And he was *mine.*

The notion, the reality as this man looked down at me, lazily stroking his cock as he watched me, was overwhelming.

GRAYSON

After removing the remnants of my clothes, I lay there, waiting.

Grayson sauntered closer, his gaze never leaving mine.

Wordlessly, I dropped to my knees, my cock throbbing with need. I sucked Grayson into my mouth, wasting no time licking and nibbling, and laving my tongue all along his shaft.

Mine, mine, mine.

Grayson sunk his fingers in my hair and pulled me up by it. It hurt, but I liked it.

It felt cathartic almost.

The pain, the pleasure.

He kissed me, his tongue running rampant in my mouth as he thrust his cock against me. I could feel the warmth of his precum spreading along my shaft, and I shuddered with desire.

"No," he said, shaking his head, his hot breath on my neck like fire. "Let me please you, baby. Let me show you how much I fucking love you," he whispered huskily against my neck.

"O... okay," I said, his words registering.

His hand wrapped around my cock, pulsing, squeezing as he pushed me back against the couch, dropping to *his* knees. He opened my legs with a force that I swear could have popped my hip out of its joint. Grayson licked the inside of my thigh, tracing lines up to my shaft.

"You're going to do exactly as I tell you, do you understand?" he asked, the command in his voice evident.

The anxiety in me ebbed. Giving up control was not easy for me, but with Grayson... I knew I could.

He would make it all okay. He would fix the broken parts of me. I wanted him to lead.

I nodded. "Yes," I said.

Grayson smirked. "Good boy," he said, and he swallowed my cock, deep-throating me in one swift move.

"Fuck!" I said, feeling my balls tighten, my orgasm already starting to form.

Grayson let up, removing his mouth from my cock, appraising me with a heated gaze as my angry cock throbbed with need. I tried to catch my breath. "Turn over," he said, his gaze darkening.

"What..."

"I said, turn over. Show me that pretty little ass of yours," he growled. "I want to taste you." His tone was all business, but there was a playfulness to it as well.

The faintest twist of his lips gave him away. "Unless... you don't want me to..."

I turned over faster than you could flip a pancake.

I absolutely wanted to, and my cock was in mutual agreement. I wanted things to be different this time.

I needed Grayson to understand how much I trusted him.

Grayson spread my cheeks almost instantly, and the onslaught of his tongue along my tight pucker, warm and wet, made me curse again. I braced myself against the couch, my legs tightening as he relentlessly licked me until I felt the faintest pressure.

I squeezed my cheeks, my thighs stiffening.

"You okay, baby?" he asked, his lustful voice tinged with concern.

I closed my eyes, arching myself back on his finger, taking a little more.

"Yes," I said, catching my breath. My leaking cock brushed against the cushions, the friction maddening.

I was so consumed with desire I didn't know if I needed to fuck my hand or be fucked. Maybe both.

"You like that?" Grayson cooed, sliding another finger in, stretching me, slowly, taking his time, letting me adjust.

I nodded as I let my forehead fall against the cushions. "Yes," I said.

I had the faintest feeling of déjà vu as my voice reverberated in my brain.

"You like that, Grayson?" I said as I slid my hand along his thigh, his legs forcing me closer, edging my cock against his entrance.

"Yes," he said, his words hazy and dark.

I gripped the back of the couch as memory spilled forth.

"Fuck," I said. I felt like the wind had been knocked out of me.

Grayson removed his fingers, his tongue probing me once more, and I cried out as another memory pushed forth.

"You're so tight," I growled, my cock pulsing as I bottomed out. I'd never heard myself like this.

I didn't know I was capable of such things...

Grayson gripped my hair, his legs locked around me like a vice, thrusting his cock against my abdomen as he cried out, bathing me in his hot release.

The emptiness I felt as I waited for him was maddening.

"Henry," Grayson's voice brought me back to the moment, and I could hear the wistfulness in it.

I turned to look over my shoulder, our gaze meeting, and I knew.

He remembered too.

"Please," I begged. I was so hard, it hurt.

"Grayson, please..." I forced the words out, the world spinning all around me.

Grayson pulled me back against his chest until he was fully inside me. The onslaught of pressure, of pain, was only temporary as he wrapped his arms around me, his right hand finding my cock, gently squeezing.

My eyes fell closed in ecstasy as he slowly dragged himself out, the pressure maddening as I waited for the fall.

"That's it," he purred, rocking back into me in a slow, torturous fashion.

"Yes," I said, leaning my head back against his shoulder. His thumb teased my wet slit as he snapped his hips against my cheeks, picking up the pace.

"Come for me, baby."

His words pushed me over the edge. I

came hard and fast, with Grayson's name on my tongue.

Warmth spread within me as his erratic thrusts stilled, as he gripped my chin and turned my face to meet his lips, swallowing my ecstatic cries with his kiss. His mouth moved against mine with grace, with a sweetness I wanted to taste over and over again.

My favorite dessert.

"Mine," I murmured against his sweet, torturous mouth.

"Mine," he whispered in repose, his lips curling into a smile as he held me, my entire body and soul coming undone in his arms.

And only when Grayson let me go, did I realize I was finally whole again.

EPILOGUE

Grayson

I LOOKED AT Henry from the passenger seat of his brand new, fully repaired Toyota. While I preferred to see him behind the wheel of my Porsche, I also knew that if we were going to do this—have a relationship—I needed to let Henry drive the car sometimes. Figuratively, and physically.

"You sure about this?" I asked.

Henry's shoulders loosened and he pursed his lips. He nodded. "Yes." His answer was solid, confident.

Ever since the other night—the night Henry finally opened up and let me in—it was like he was a different person.

Not as tense, not as scared.

I reached out to take his hand, squeezing it with support. "Okay then, let's go have ourselves a gay old time, baby," I teased.

Henry let go of my hand, opening the door, and I did the same.

It didn't take long to find Giselle, who was in the center of the room occupying three high top tables. The party was there, plus Drew and the florist.

"Hey guys, I'm so glad you could make it," Giselle said, giving us both warm hugs.

Henry hugged her back genuinely. "Hey."

"Aaron's angling for a rematch," Mia said as she hugged her brother.

"A rematch?" I asked, looking between them.

Henry let go of her, rolling his eyes. "It's nothing, just—"

"Henry scored the winning point that other night when we faced off in the billiards," Giselle shrugged. "I told him I'd love to see him whoop your ass in a game, and then when Aaron heard you both were coming..."

"What do you say, Gray? You up for a

challenge?" Aaron cracked a smile over his beer.

I shot my boyfriend—God, I still felt my damn heart race every time I called him that—a dirty look.

"You think you can beat me?" I asked, licking my lips. I hoped Henry would take my bait.

And he did. Like the good boy he was.

He brattily flipped his dark hair out of his eyes, shrugging. "I know I can," he said.

Oh, it's on, baby.

"I will hold you to that," I said, as Aaron fist pumped the air.

"Yes! Gray's on my team!" he hollered.

"Then Henry's on mine, " Riley rebutted.

"I hate to break it to you, guys, but it looks like the table's taken," Julie pointed to the corner.

I could see a group of three men hanging out, not playing, but taking up the space nonetheless. Riley crossed his arms.

"Well, we'll just have to ask them nicely to move." Aaron shrugged, chugging the remains of his beer. "Or we'll have to challenge them. Winner takes the table."

"I'm down with that," Henry said, interjecting.

The smile that formed on my face was impossible to hide. I slid my arm around Henry's shoulders, pulling him close, my lips at his ear.

"Winner takes the loser in the backseat of your car," I whispered, knowing it would throw him off.

Henry cast me a sly look. "I'm going to make you swallow that promise," he whispered back, grinning wickedly.

"I'm counting on it, baby," I said as he slid his arm around my waist, and we walked toward the billiards knowing we'd already won the game.

Because as far as I was concerned, there was no greater victory than happily ever after.

Thank you for reading Grayson and Henry's story.

If you enjoyed this book, please return to your favorite retailer and leave a review. Even a few words could mean the world to an author.

Continue the series with Riley's story, Book 5 in Jasper Springs!

OTHER BOOKS BY EVIE

Federal Protection Agency
Mason
Rafe
Ryzen
Cooper
Noah
Damien
Sebastian
Gabe
Logan

Ruthless Empire
Courting Danger
Chasing Danger
Kissing Danger

Smokejumpers
Hawke
Cyrus
Jase
Gage
Jackson
Xavier

Jasper Springs
Cade
Dawson
Drew
Grayson
Riley
Mitch

From The Edge
Shattered
Runaway
Jaded
Rescue
Hidden
Tormented

Gray Vale Pack
His Fated Mate
His Wounded Warrior
His Healing Heart

ABOUT THE AUTHOR

Evie Riley is a prolific, neurodivergent author known for her captivating MM romance novels. She has gained a significant following and topped the LGBT+ action and adventure bestseller charts with her series.

Evie's writing style often explores dark and gritty themes where her men must overcome difficult obstacles in their search for love, but she has also ventured into sweeter small-town romances, incorporating tropes like enemies-to-lovers, friends-to-lovers, age-gap, and forced proximity. She is known for crafting engaging romantic suspense novels and has a knack for creating interconnected series worlds that keep readers invested.

Interestingly, Ms. Riley has hinted at exploring new genres, such as Alien Omegaverse Romance, in the future.

Outside of writing, she enjoys spending time at the beach and has a quirky personality, described by her partner as ranging from cute to deadly, depending on her blood-chocolate levels.

Evie spends her nights writing bad boys in love, and her days wrangling the sweet boys she loves.